Secret of the Grand Canyon

Secret of the Grand Canyon

The Adventures of Tyler Young and the Warriors

G. C. Grange

First Printing, 2023

Edited by Kerry Nierenberg

CONTENTS

INTRODUCTION

Travel with Tyler Young and the Warriors on a fascinating, action-packed journey through Arizona's deep canyons and caverns in search of nature's hidden secrets and long-forgotten Indian caves. Join these indomitable adventurers as they brave the elements and encounter not only jaguars, rattlesnakes, bighorn sheep, and eagles, but an evil man eager to avenge a long-standing grudge, and even Ice-Age creatures. The adventure leads into the Grand Canyon, one of the largest canyons on earth, and to its largest side canyon, home of the "people of the blue-green waters," the Havasupai Indians.

Secret of the Grand Canyon illustrates the natural world in authentic detail within a powerfully alluring fictional tale. Embedded in this story of adventure is information on hiking, climbing, caving, camping, and safe environmental practices. Also sprinkled in are explanations about the history, natural history, plants, and animals in the rugged state of Arizona. The desert, canyon, and mountain landscapes portrayed are etched with striking accuracy; their descriptions come from the author's personal experience in this wild country.

The forces driving these characters are the natural instincts in most humans: curiosity, exploration, and discovery. To satisfy these urges, the adventurers challenge their muscles and senses on a quest to discover the wonders of nature and to unravel mysteries of our ancient human ancestors.

Eagle Petroglyph
Pete Connolly

1

The Mummy Cave

Searching for natural wonders through heat and cold
makes us strong, tough, and bold.
Up the hills our legs must pound
until true Warriors we are crowned.
Discovering secrets not yet told,
observing evidence of the old.
Concealed deep beneath the ground,
hidden treasures still not found.

They struggled up the steep rock to look in every cave and crevice, searching for the lost mummy cave of the Hohokam. Climbing up the dome-shaped granite mountain and pushing Tyler's dog Beau up a vertical cliff in their path, Colter and Shawnee, a boy and girl of fourteen, decided to explore an interesting shallow cave. A wreath of small desert ferns grew at the entrance.

"Hey, over here!" they yelled upon finding large pieces of pottery in the sand of the cave floor.

Makoa, fifteen, ran over to join them. Running his hand through the sand, he too found a stone tool. The mindful kids left everything where it was found. Now the adventurers knew that they were possibly on the right track. Tyler, guide and leader, looked down from the top of the cliff and smiled, acknowledging their finds.

This tough group had grown up hiking and exploring Arizona and often liked to call themselves the "Apaches" in honor of that famous tribe. Tyler Young, a middle-aged man, youthful by nature, led the way. His passion was the adventure of exploring beautiful, untamed wilderness, while always keeping an eye out for signs of long-gone inhabitants. As a little boy, he had wanted to live like the Indians of the Southwest; as an adult he tracked their ancient signs.

Today, Tyler and the three teenagers were climbing a steep granite mountain north of Tucson, above a prehistoric Hohokam village that had been inhabited from about 800 to more than 1,000 years ago. High peaks with jagged summits loomed on three sides, and to the north the desert stretched away for miles. Their hike from a basecamp had started along a creek on the valley floor near the village's crumbling rock walls. Boulder hopping along the water, they entered the canyon from which the stream emerged, following it for a while and then branching off to climb the surrounding peaks.

Tyler had heard stories from his dad, a retired archeologist, about rumors from some old-time cowboys of a Hohokam mummy cave somewhere in this remote corner of the mountains. Hohokam means "all gone" and comes from their more recent ancestors, the Pima. Such a cave would be very rare, but he had finally decided to search for it despite having few clues; the old cowboys' memories had faded with time.

The fascinating Hohokam culture spread through much of southern Arizona into Mexico, with their populations concentrated around the Gila and Salt River valleys in the Phoenix area and in the Tucson Basin. The Hohokam culture is renowned for its art and rich ceremonial life. Their large-scale irrigation agriculture, incorporating a huge canal system, was the most advanced in North America with hundreds of square miles of fields. An extensive trade network brought seashells and macaw feathers from Mexico. Today, these artifacts are still found at Hohokam sites, as are ball courts, also influenced by the great southern civilizations of Mesoamerica.

Tyler and the three "Warriors," as he called them, had come across several grinding stones or metates left behind by the Hohokam or possibly earlier hunters and gatherers known as the Archaic people.

Along the creek they had seen these large flat granite rocks with depressions as deep as eight inches from years of grinding. They followed a draw with a game trail that led away from the creek and up the rugged side of the canyon to a hanging valley where higher-elevation oak trees mixed with the giant saguaro cacti. More metates were found.

The Warriors rubbed their hands over the smooth rock as Tyler explained, "Native Americans probably used these to process the acorns and mesquite beans in this valley. Mesquite flour from the beans and pods has always been a favorite food of Southwestern tribes."

After a few more paces, he pointed and exclaimed, "Hey, there's a mano over there!" Tyler walked over and picked up a hand-sized smooth rock – an example of one used to grind the acorns or beans on the metates.

The group made their way up the tall peak, continuing to search for the lost Indian cave until reaching the top. They paused to look out over the mountains. A giant golden eagle soared up in front of them from around a cliff, releasing an ear-piercing scream. Its war cry, deeper and greater in volume than any hawk's, filled Tyler and the Warriors with awe. The eagle was not only magnificent, but a sacred bird to all Native Americans: "carrying their prayers high to the heavens."

All eyes watched intently as the great bird soared across the canyon and flapped higher into the jagged peaks. The adventurers followed the eagle's progress until finally it disappeared, blending into the dark trees, and there they saw something that would change their lives forever.

"Look!" said Tyler. "Where we lost him, that black hole. It looks like a cave in the rocks on the edge of those trees! Want to climb that peak and have a look?"

The Warriors were pondering the ascent of the rugged-looking hillside of brush, rocks, and cliffs. Meanwhile, Tyler optimistically prepared to get underway, always willing to see an adventure to the end.

For Tyler, difficult wilderness travel was a normal occurrence. From boyhood he had grown up on the edge of wild lands and had taken long hikes up the canyons and through the hills with his brothers. His dad, the archeologist, had taken him along on many digs in the back country. He had known the solitude of the mountains and canyons and had heard their solemn echoes. As individuals learn to engage with the dangers of the wilderness, a self-confidence grows that is readily apparent. There was about him an Indian's courage, a natural pride or dignity.

Tyler couldn't stay away from wilderness exploration. Something called to him in a loud, clear voice, and he yearned for it with a vast hunger not easily satisfied. Listening to that voice, traveling and hiking all around the western United States, and dreaming of seeing the whole world's wild and beautiful places kept his adventure spirit alive. A persistent hunger for knowledge about the prehistoric people who had lived in the areas he explored also occupied his mind. Time spent in the wilderness observing the signs left from these interesting, mystical people and knowledge from his father granted him a great deal of insight. He felt intrigued and obsessed with their lifestyle, and if granted one wish, he would go back and live with the native people of the past.

"Maybe the eagle's showing us the way to the mummy cave," Makoa said.

That helped decide it; they'd all give the ascent a try. Huffing and puffing, they climbed the steep, rocky slope, avoided cactus, and with great effort pushed through thick stands of catclaw acacia with its sharp, curved thorns. It was impossible not to get scratched or have their clothes torn, but they were all used to this and accepted it as a necessary part of exploring.

Walking near an old, gnarled oak, Shawnee saw a red-, white- and black-ringed snake curled up like a necklace on an extending root.

She cried, "A king snake! Come look!" The snake sprang for cover, but Tyler's quick hands succeeded in catching hold of the smooth body. The snake remained calm as they admired its colors.

Tyler pointed out, "It's a Sonoran Mountain king snake, often confused with venomous coral snakes. The North American variety of coral snake has red rings bordered by yellow or cream-colored rings, but not all the coral snake species in the world have this color pattern.

"Remember the old saying," said Tyler. "Red next to black, friends to Jack; red next to yellow, kill a fellow. And that's only true in North America!" He bent down and gently let the snake go.

Resuming their ascent, Beau, Tyler's mountain-hardy cocker spaniel, moved easily through the rough terrain, leading the way. He would often come across animals – usually rabbits, but sometimes deer or fox – and enjoy a short chase before the swifter wild ones would lose him.

Seeing something white through the brush, Makoa, leaned down to pick it up and exclaimed, "An antler!"

"Nice find," Tyler said.

"It's a four-pointer," Makoa said excitedly with a broad smile. "My second one. Someday I'll have a collection like you, Tyler."

Climbing upward, they soon approached the dark hole seen from below. The deep black seemed to indicate that it might go back into the mountain, but they also knew it could be just a deep shadow from an overhang. Beneath it was a steep twenty-foot cliff. Tyler, with years of climbing experience, moved smoothly up the rock, cautiously testing each handhold and foothold to make sure they were secure before moving his full weight onto them. He moved just one arm or leg at a time; the other three limbs he left firmly planted should a hold break free. Reaching the cave mouth and crouching at the entrance, eagerly anticipating what might lie ahead, he immediately saw petroglyphs chipped into the rock around him. His heart began to beat faster.

"Petroglyphs!" he yelled. "There's one of Kokopelli and a lizard symbol. We've definitely found an Indian cave." Going a few yards farther initiated deep feelings of adventure, but it was too black to see, so he went back to retrieve his flashlight and help his friends up the cliff with a short rope he had in his pack.

"What's a Kokopelli?" asked Colter.

"It's the name given to the image of a bent-over or hump-backed flute player," said Tyler as he looked in his pack for a flashlight. "Kokopelli is seen mostly in the Four Corners region of Utah, Colorado, New Mexico, and Arizona.

He's thought to have been a fertility figure, a traveling trader who announced his arrival with his flute. The hump on his back possibly represents a bag of seeds, and he may have been a fertility figure for all life – plants, animals, as well as humans.

"So, he represents regeneration of life," Colter pointed out wisely.

"Yup, and he's generally associated with well-being, both spiritual and physical," Tyler explained while securing himself to the cliff with some webbing wrapped around a large boulder.

Makoa threw one end of their rope up to Tyler, then tied himself to the other end and started to ascend. Strong, tan, and lean, he climbed the rock face easily as Tyler took slack out of the rope, ready to catch a fall (what climbers call belaying). Reaching the cave, Makoa grinned at the sight of the petroglyphs; his dark shoulder-length hair framed his gleaming smile.

Colter, the stoutest of the group, prepared to climb next as Makoa untied the rope from his waist and threw that end down. Built with large, strong muscles, Colter climbed athletically and smoothly, almost effortlessly, with the security of Tyler belaying him.

Shawnee tied up Beau at the bottom of the cliff, and at Tyler's request, poured some water into a depression in the rock for him. Then she took her turn tying the rope around her waist and started climbing with her long black hair blowing in the wind.

Stopping by a small ledge to look closely at something, her beautiful dark eyes flashed excitedly as she blurted out, "A turquoise bead! It's perfectly shaped." She put it in her mouth for safekeeping and continued climbing.

All three teenagers were strong climbers, well-muscled, tanned, and healthy from years of traveling in the wilderness. Their legs felt like steel from miles of rugged hiking, and their arms resembled pythons. The wilderness, with its sometimes uncomfortable weather and difficult terrain, had strengthened their character far beyond their years and had given them a greater ability to endure hardships. They grew to love the natural world, eagerly sought out adventure and excitement, and valued exploring enchanting wonderlands.

The Warriors stood together at the mouth of the cave, amazed at the turquoise bead Shawnee had found. Tyler coiled the rope while the others dug flashlights out of their packs. After checking all the lights, Tyler led the way into the natural tunnel.

Meanwhile, down in the shadows of the valley below, a lithe figure was coming up the difficult rocky canyon bottom, rapidly jumping from rock to rock, moving as someone does who has a purpose and knows where he's going. The hiker, sporting a turquoise headband, day pack, and a walking staff made from a saguaro rib, paused to look up at the cliffs where Tyler and the Warriors had gone.

Moving beyond the cave entrance and between two tall stalagmites that formed an enchanting gate, the explorers could see a small pond. Water dripped steadily into it from the stalactites hanging above, producing sounds like a marimba or xylophone. They cautiously crossed to the other side of the pool and looked back across the water, taking a moment to enjoy the beautiful scene with reflected light from the entrance. Eager to keep exploring, they continued deeper into the cave.

The figure in the canyon below continued traveling at a steady pace. When met with a pool where the cliffs and rocks made it too difficult to get around, the athlete threw the walking stick like a spear toward the other side and slipped into the water, holding the pack overhead with one arm. Swimming smoothly across, the intrepid traveler continued with the ease and steadiness of one long used to wilderness travel.

Back in the cave, Tyler and the Warriors walked, crouched over, through a narrow passage for another 50 feet to the edge of a dark pit. The tunnel ended at this obstacle, and it seemed this would be the end of their exploring, but looking over the edge, they could see an old wooden ladder.

"Wait here!" said Tyler excitedly, climbing down to a ledge where he could reach the ladder. "I'll check it out and see if it's safe."

"Don't trust it," warned Makoa.

Examining the ladder closely, Tyler observed aloud, "The rungs seem to be tied with yucca fibers. I don't know if they'll hold. Looks like it was made a long time ago, perhaps even hundreds of years. This is really old juniper. We better rig up a safety rope in case it gives out."

Tyler came back up and tied on to the end of the rope while Colter, being the largest, anchored himself to a sturdy stalagmite and prepared to belay him. Tyler then climbed carefully down the rickety ladder which held his weight, and the rope was just long enough for him to reach the last rung. He stepped down onto a thick ledge that appeared to be 30 feet above the bottom of the pit. Looking into the area below, most of which was cut off from view, Tyler thought there could possibly be a larger room, but it was hard to tell. He peered over the ledge and noticed small footholds cut into the rock wall.

"I think I can make it down," he said. His fingers and toes fit perfectly into the worn, old holds as he made his way to the floor of the pit. Next, Colter belayed Shawnee and Makoa down to the ledge; each of them managed the primitively cut steps without a problem. Then

Colter hooked up his gear and rappelled to the ledge and the very end of the rope, unhooked himself, and successfully climbed down.

Moving on, a large stalagmite blocked the view, but as they passed around it, a cry of astonishment rang out at what their lights revealed. A wave of half-hysterical delight shot through Tyler. Eyes gleaming, his face lit up as if a fire burned within. Before them was something few modern people have ever seen: an ancient Indian burial chamber.

Along the wall were seven dried bodies sitting on a narrow ledge, tied to short poles wedged into the rock. The skin had withered and dried in the arid climate; hard leather had drawn tight over the cheekbones. The skulls appeared as hideous as one can imagine: teeth broken out, jaws askew, and long hair still attached in many places. Hanging upon the bodies were beautiful turquoise necklaces and pendants of shell and crystals. Most of the mummies had seashell bracelets. One donned a woven headband of beads with a design like a jaguar, and all wore yucca-fiber sandals.

This discovery was extremely rare. The Hohokam usually cremated their dead, often putting the ashes in pots or simply burying them. These individuals must have been very important, perhaps chiefs or medicine men.

In between the mummies rested large, beautifully painted pots with intricate designs. Paintings decorated the walls, and perhaps most amazing of all was a bright shaft of light beaming in from a small crack in the roof of the cave. Incredibly, the light shaft, known as a "sun dagger," struck the rock wall in the center of a spiraling circular petroglyph. Tyler had read of these sun daggers before, and the petroglyphs they shone on were usually lined up within natural rock formations or constructed houses and designed to signal the spring or fall equinox.

Amazed, Tyler spoke up, "Today is March 21st. I can't believe we've found this cave on the vernal equinox, just in time to see the dagger of light hit the center of the spiral!"

"Look at this!" Colter shouted, dipping his hands into one of the pots. "Dozens of quartz crystal arrowheads!"

"This one's filled with turquoise beads!" Makoa cried.

Shawnee placed the bead she found in among the others. Looking into the next pot, she exclaimed with great delight, "Seashells! Some of them are carved with designs and animal shapes...and there's bracelets and pendants in this one."

Tyler pitched in, "The Hohokam were the first culture found to etch shells using fermented fruit juice from cactus. This makes a weak acid that eats the shell partly away where it's not covered with pitch, or sap."

"I get it. You paint on the pitch to create the design you want," concluded Shawnee.

"Exactly."

Looking through the pots, often holding up an artifact for the bright sun dagger to illuminate, kept them intensely busy. They marveled at the magical sheen of the crystal arrowheads, some with fractures that appeared to contain all the colors of the rainbow. They also found beautiful abalone shell pendants, along with bone rings and ivory-like bone awls polished from years of use.

"Look at these pictures," Makoa said as he wandered toward the wall. Pictographs had been painted in various shades of red, white, black, and brown. A large, angular red snake crossed the middle of the wall. The scattered mural featured pictures of deer, bighorn sheep, and humans, but the most impressive image was a large petroglyph of an eagle with outstretched wings chipped deep into the rock. The group spent two full hours looking around the room in wonder before finally sitting down for a meeting and snack.

"This is incredible," Tyler said. "We'll leave it exactly as it is. This stuff is much more meaningful here than anywhere else."

"It's also a sacred burial," said Makoa. "It would be illegal, and wrong, to take anything."

"I think we should hide the entrance better when we leave," added Shawnee.

The youngsters sighed as they continued to look in wonder and envy at all the artifacts.

Tyler assured them, “Don’t worry. This will stay our secret, and we’ll come back together to see it.”

"These beautiful things belong here and look so much better hidden in this cave high in the mountains," said Colter, who had always been very caring and sensitive. "We are the luckiest people in the whole world."

The Warriors and Tyler made a pact that nobody else would be shown the cave, unless otherwise agreed to by all. After munching on a snack of dried fruit and nuts, they decided to go outside and camouflage the opening before heading back to their camp.

After climbing up the cut steps below the ladder, Tyler reached for the ledge and began to pull himself up. Suddenly it broke away! Flying back off the wall with debris falling about, he still held on to the largest section of rock.

He managed to miraculously push it down between his legs so it wouldn’t crush him. Landing first on his feet, he then fell back onto the loose rock. Thanks to reflexes honed from years of wilderness dangers, Tyler was not seriously hurt.

The kids had luckily been standing off to the side and also escaped injury. After brushing himself off, Tyler contemplated how to get up to the ladder and their rope. The main part of the ledge above the footsteps was gone. The ladder rested on a small bit of rock that remained, but below it he now faced four feet of bare cliff.

The Warriors took turns supporting each other in trying to reach the ladder or rope from the top two rock steps, but they could not get close enough. After quickly surveying the room, it became obvious that nothing inside might help them get up past the smooth rock section. The poles holding the mummies in place had grown weak with age and seemed too thin and short in any case. They soon realized they were trapped and settled back away from the dried bodies to sit and think. Frightful images began to grow in their minds at the thought of the darkness that would eventually overtake them. They turned off their flashlights to save batteries.

Shawnee, always light-hearted and easygoing, said, "We'll get out somehow. I know it." Her optimism helped keep the others from experiencing panic, a feeling which can spread faster than fire in dry grass. Tyler decided to light one of the candles he had brought; the single steady flame had the same effect as Shawnee's words in dispelling their fear, at least for the moment.

Tyler dove deeply into thought and apprehension about their predicament until Makoa suddenly declared, "We can chop steps in the rock like the Hohokam did!"

"That might be possible," Tyler responded, "but it looks like pretty hard rock and will probably take a long time. That said...I think you're right. It could be our only chance."

Having no other alternative, they looked for something to use as a hammer. The situation seemed hopeless given how solid the rock felt, but the only option left was to try. The arduous task would keep them occupied during the stressful time ahead, however, this effort would also burn precious calories: a dangerous trade off.

Scouting around, they came across materials to make a stone hammer. Makoa found a short and hopefully strong enough stick for the handle.

Colter stumbled on a sawtooth-edged scraping tool left by the Hohokam that could be used to split the stick for the hammer head. Shawnee found a pretty good hammer rock of basalt that looked like the proper shape for tying into the split stick. In fact, it came across as if maybe the rock had been brought into this cave for that very purpose hundreds of years ago. They had no sinew or deer tendon which the Indians would have used, but their shoelaces would do to tie the hammer rock to the stick.

Keeping busy lessened their fears, but the same question lingered in each of their minds, 'How long will it take to make a step in the solid rock?'

Taking the sturdy, well-made tool, Tyler worked his way up to the last two holds where he could stand and started hammering away at the rock. Several minutes later he had made a small indentation. Even knowing that the work would go slowly, perhaps too slowly, they took turns with the hammer and kept at it.

The day wore on, and the light coming through the tiny hole in the roof began to fade as sunset rapidly approached. The hammering continued in a painfully slow manner, and the size of the first hold barely increased. The Warriors were growing tired, and Tyler began to make mental calculations as to how long their food, water, and flashlights would last.

If only the pool in the upper part of the cave drained down to them, then their situation might not have been quite so dire. After looking in all the corners and cracks, they could find no trace of the precious liquid. Each of them brought a small flashlight, though one had already failed. Tyler also packed two candles, though the first was burnt halfway down after being used.

All felt the seriousness of their situation, but they worked on pounding the hammer into the rock without expressing their worries, clinging to this only hope of escape. Fear made them feel hollow and empty inside, and as the mental pressures mounted, Tyler's head ached between the temples, as if in a clamp.

Below the cave entrance, still tied to the tree, Beau began to feel worried and lonely. As dusk started to close in on the mountains, he began howling for his friends. The Warriors could just barely hear the mournful sound and hoped that someone else might hear it too, eventually coming to find them. Despite their positive hopes, these seasoned explorers reasoned that little chance of such a rescue existed in this location so far off the beaten path.

Noticing the deepening shadows, the solitary traveler in the canyon below had turned to head back but stopped as Beau's barely audible howls descended from the heights. Looking up with intense interest, scanning the upper ridges and peaks, and listening to the mournful cries from up high, the alert hiker turned and started up the canyon with renewed energy. This 'sound tracker' left the canyon bottom and climbed the long, steep, and rugged slope, meeting obstacles with increased speed and strength and leaping over boulders with the agility of a mountain lion. Closer and closer the climber progressed toward the howling dog, ultimately ending up within a hundred yards of the cave as dusk deepened. Beau fell silent as he listened to the person approaching through the underbrush, but when he saw the hiker's form emerging from the foliage, he barked hysterically, his guardian instincts coming into full play.

Hearing Beau's intense barking filled Tyler and the Warriors with mixed feelings of hope for rescue and worry of wild animals attacking the dog. They whooped and shouted for help, but since it was now dark and the rugged terrain so inaccessible, they doubted that any human would be nearing the cave.

"Maybe it's a mountain lion," worried Tyler.

They sat and listened until the barking stopped, then continued yelling for help, but heard nothing and soon gave up, figuring that whatever had upset Beau ended up leaving the area. Tyler and the Warriors took a rest before sending someone up the steps to work again. Suddenly, they heard faint sounds coming from the tunnel above. Colter and Shawnee yelled again for help, but no reply followed. Instinctively wary, everyone hid quietly behind rocks then froze in place.

Soon, leaning over the lip of the pit and clutching a flashlight, appeared the strong, lithe figure who had so rapidly ascended from the canyon below. Beau emerged alongside her and stayed close to her legs, fearful of the cave. Recognizing Sierra, Tyler's soulmate, they all let out cries of delight.

"A fine mess you've gotten yourself into this time, Tyler," she chuckled. "You're darn lucky I found you."

"Yeah, we are," Tyler replied. "What are you doing here? How did you find us? I thought you were going fishing with your dad in Mexico."

"Well, the trip got canceled this morning. I got bored and decided to come looking for you."

"I'm sure glad I saw you last night and told you where we were going."

"Me too," said Sierra. "I was heading back home when I heard Beau barking. I'd recognize that bark anywhere, so I followed it up here. What happened? How'd you get down there?"

Sierra was Tyler's girlfriend and hiking partner of many years, so without hesitation, Tyler told her what they'd found, "...but then the ledge below the ladder broke off! That's how we got trapped. The bottom twenty feet of cliff has crude steps cut into it, so we only need about six more feet of rope."

Sierra suggested finding a strong branch to use for a ladder, but she knew it would be hard to find one long enough. She went to have a look outside.

Trying to think of a solution, Tyler started walking toward the mummies. His eyes wandered to their sandals and the tough yucca fibers used to fabricate them.

Suddenly he yelled, "Sierra, wait! If you don't find a branch long enough, maybe collect a bundle of yucca. We'll make a strong rope in less time than it would take you to run home for one. We could tie it to the end of our other rope."

"You think so?" Sierra answered. "There's a lot of yucca on the slope outside. Let's try it."

Realizing that it would be very hard, especially at night, to find a long enough branch from one of the gnarled oak trees growing at this elevation, Sierra started cutting off the two-foot yucca 'leaves.' She cut only a few from each base, so as not to destroy the whole plant, then carried a bundle of leaves into the cave, threw them to Tyler, and went back for more.

The Warriors found rocks to use as scrapers and went to work scraping the green flesh from the long, pointed yucca pieces, exposing the plant's string-like fibers. Soon they had amassed a pile of the two-foot-long fibrous sections, and Tyler began braiding the lengths together. After a few hours, they completed crafting a double-thick rope measuring six feet. Testing it with a good tug proved it was strong enough to hold their weight. Tyler threw the yucca line up to Sierra, who tied it securely to the other rope with a double fisherman's knot.

Sierra expressed an eagerness to see the burial chamber, but Tyler first wanted to get someone else on top for safety. Shawnee offered; she climbed up and waited patiently with Beau, safely tied to a stalagmite. Sierra descended into the chamber and looked around like an excited child on Christmas.

She stared intently in amazement at the mummified Indians, turned toward Tyler, and in a high-pitched voice said, "You've found it! You've actually found it!"

For a moment they stood together in awe. Then Tyler brought out the second candle and placed it in front of the mummies, illuminating the amazing scene even more.

Recognizing the late hour, he said, "I think we ought to just spend the night here. It's warm now, and we still have enough of the flashlights working to get us through until morning."

"Why not?" said Sierra. "This will be great! And probably safer."

"I'm exhausted," Makoa said. "I'd much rather sleep here than hike back to camp tonight."

Colter, nodding, said nothing but looked sheepishly at the mummies. He went over to ask Shawnee what she thought. She looked down from the top of the ladder and agreed that it would be better to spend the night there.

She noted, “We can get water from the pool above us.”

Then Colter loudly added a condition, “I’m OK with that...if we have a candle burning, all night.”

Tyler climbed up again to double-check the rope, then asked the others to help "spot" Shawnee as she easily lowered herself hand over hand down the yucca rope and rock steps. Everyone passed up water bottles for Tyler to fill, then he untied Beau and said they were going for a quick look outside.

As he exited the cave, he flicked off his light to see the stars while Beau searched around. Confronted at first with total blackness, his eyes soon adjusted. Stars began to appear, next the Milky Way glistened, and finally the outlines of distant peaks and canyon ridge-tops came into view. Gradually the stars became even more brilliant, sparkling different colors in the clear mountain sky. As Tyler watched the whole night scene manifest, he thought about how often people's impressions of nature resemble the way in which nightfall had just been revealed to him.

At first, raw wilderness can appear harsh, forbidding, and mysterious, but if you merely stay, look, and listen, you might observe new, simple, and wonderful things. 'It's the same with getting to know people,' he thought. He compared the depths of human beings and the depths of the wild, and at the same time, he briefly pondered his wonder and almost equal need for both.

Just then, a shooting star blazed across the sky. Tyler smiled and let out a sigh. He called Beau back to the cave, tied him securely for the night at the top of the pit, and climbed back down to the burial chamber.

Before long, everyone had settled in, using their packs and extra clothes as pillows and blankets. The candlelight played around the extraordinary primitive scene as the adventurers stared in wonder and appreciation at their discovery. Lined up in front of them were the seven mummies, the beautifully painted pots in between, and the picto-graphs and petroglyphs dancing on the walls from the single wavering flame. While they observed this incredible display of mystical antiquity, a strong silence fell over them. Tyler's eyes shone in the candlelight. The shadows of the Hohokam mummies moved on the wall as if alive. Spell-bound, no one spoke. Then, for some mysterious reason, their gaze turned to the eagle petroglyph.

In the candlelight, the eagle looked like it was flying. Tyler giggled with delight but then let the silence take hold again, hoping the Warriors had noticed the same subtle visual show. He looked at the breast of the eagle, the carved lines made to appear like feathers, and the intersecting natural crack. The flickering candle caused these lines to move, making Tyler think of flowing water.

The pattern drew in his whole consciousness as he began to fade toward sleep. Falling into a dream-like state, he imagined the lines to be winding rivers through valleys and canyons. Abruptly, he felt a rush of inspiration as his eyes came to rest on an arrowhead symbol mysteriously placed among these carved lines and cracks. Emerging with a jolt from his trance, Tyler instinctively felt the secret of the mummy cave being revealed.

"Is that a map?" he blurted out.

Startled, his companions asked, "Where?"

Tyler stood up and walked toward the wall, pointing to the eagle's chest.

He demonstrated, "These cracks incorporated into the petroglyph look like the map of a river system. I've seen what looked like petroglyph maps before on canyon walls in Utah and southwestern Colorado, but here they've utilized a natural crack. I wonder what this arrowhead means."

"If it's a map, maybe the arrowhead marks something," wondered Colter.

"Who knows? Maybe a ceremonial site," answered Makoa.

"It could lead to a special clay bank or a good obsidian or flint site for stone tools," added Shawnee.

"Or even another cave," Tyler guessed. "I'll copy it in the morning, and we'll study it later."

The tired adventurers resumed their attempts to sleep on the hard floor and quietly observed the scene.

Getting bored, Colter spoke up, "Tyler, tell us about the Apaches and Geronimo. Do you think it's true that the Apaches could run all day?"

Tyler started telling stories, some of which the Warriors had heard many times before. They let their imaginations run free with the Apaches, never growing tired of these tales of the well-known Southwestern tribe.

"Yes, they say Apache Warriors used to be able to run 70 miles or more in 24 hours, often with women and children. Geronimo, one of the most famous Warriors in history, and the other last free Apaches traveled great distances through the roughest country in the Southwest to strike or keep ahead of the U.S. Cavalry and the Mexican Army."

Shawnee spoke up. "Geronimo loved this country, didn't he?"

Tyler paused, then said, "He sure did. In old age he wanted very badly to go back to his homeland, but he was never allowed because of local public sentiment. He had destroyed many ranches and raided them for supplies as he fled reservation life. Geronimo and many other great Warriors fought bravely against two powerful governments, Mexico and the United States.

"These natives had tried desperately to keep their land, game, and freedom, and raiding and war remained a strong element of the Indian culture. Geronimo came from a branch of the Chiricahua Apaches; living among the rugged mountains of Southern Arizona, New Mexico, and Northern Mexico. This tough tribe was the last Apache group to be subdued. For a while, the tragic clash of cultures caused many on both sides to hate and fight each other."

"Geronimo was one of the greatest fighters," prompted Makoa.

"He sure was," Tyler continued. "Muscular and stocky, with a sharp-eyed look of power and determination, some called him the 'human tiger.' During battle he was fearless, often jumping into the middle of the action and ripping men from their saddles. Geronimo's god figure Usen told him in a dream that he would not die from a bullet. Wounded at least 28 times from gunshots, knives, and sabers, he still lived to be an old man. But he sure wasn't the only great Indian warrior; there were many others."

Sierra relaxed and enjoyed listening to Tyler teaching and interacting with his protégés, telling stories about the Apaches.

He went on to tell tales of other great warriors and leaders from the Chiricahuas and various bands of the Apache tribes that lived in Arizona, New Mexico, and Northern Mexico: Mangas Coloradas, Cochise and his son Naiche, Victorio, Juh, Yanosha, Fun, Loco, Nana, Perico, Chihuahua, Kaahteney, Eskiminzin, Massai, and even the grandson of Cochise, Niño.

Tyler shared more, "Niño Cochise escaped into the Sierra Madre of Mexico and lived a warrior's life before becoming an actor in Los Angeles, then a crop-dusting pilot. He lived to be 101! The 110-year-old medicine man with him in Mexico was the same medicine man of his father, Naiche. Amazingly, he had also treated his grandfather, the great leader of the Chiricuahua Apaches named Cochise. Apache leaders like Cochise and Mangas and the people of their tribes were at times very friendly and tolerant of the pioneers moving west, until their survival and way of life was at stake."

The kids then wanted to hear about the training of a young warrior.

"Well," Tyler went on, "at age six or younger a boy might have used a bow and arrow to bring down small game such as birds, rabbits, and squirrels, but serious training began at eight. A young warrior would be required to climb to the top of a mountain and back before sunrise – often following a plunge in a freezing creek. Young Apaches were instructed that 'your legs are your friends' and would train in endurance runs, sometimes with a mouthful of water they weren't allowed to swallow until the end. Geronimo himself often helped teach them; Niño Cochise remembers Geronimo being a bit hard. Once, after playing a practical joke on Geronimo, he was thrown up onto a stout bush.

"Apaches were experts with spears and the bow. They could shoot arrows, occasionally poisoned, with amazing speed and accuracy from many yards away. Boys often practiced fighting in small groups against each other using arrows without points, dulled spears, and leather rock-throwing slings. Injuries often resulted from these training fights, toughening the upcoming Warriors. Then there were games of accuracy with bows and arrows. In one game, a boy would shoot an arrow into a dirt bank; his opponent would try to hit or cross the first arrow with his shot, to win both arrows. In another game, one would shoot as high as he could – almost straight up, then see how many other arrows could be loaded and fired before the first one hit the ground.

"They were also vigorously trained in horsemanship. Once a child could ride bareback, they would practice jumping, riding up and down steep slopes, navigating through brush, and leaning to the side to grab objects from the ground."

"Awesome," Shawnee put in.

"Creep and freeze games and versions of hide and seek helped them develop the stalking skills necessary in their style of guerrilla warfare. For the final part of training, a boy had to complete a two-day cross-country run without food or sleep. Finally, to become a full warrior, an Apache must perform well in four war or raiding expeditions. Geronimo reached warrior status at seventeen years of age.

"Equally necessary for survival was their knowledge of the land and where to find water. They knew the locations of small springs and where to dig at the bottom of mountains in the dry canyons or washes to find the life-sustaining liquid. There were many other great Warriors, but Geronimo became so well-known because he was on the run for so long, traversing the most rugged mountains and canyons of the Southwest with unbelievable endurance and stealth in avoiding capture.

"The Chiricahua Apaches believed that certain people, including Geronimo, had the power to make themselves invisible and to foretell natural occurrences or where the soldiers would appear. Time after time, the soldiers in chase would swear their quarry had 'melted' into the landscape. Geronimo was a respected shaman for the 'powers' he often exhibited, and some opposed or feared him for his intensity and commitment to freedom. He was also a successful healer and medicine man for his people, needless to say a complex person," Tyler concluded.

After savoring the stories about the Apaches, the Warriors began talking among themselves about the different Indian feats they'd heard. Meanwhile, Tyler told Sierra every detail of discovering the mummy cave, and eventually their conversation turned back to the eagle petroglyph with the curious arrowhead on its chest.

Sierra shook her head. "If that's a map, Tyler, your treasure hunt or wild goose chase is just beginning. Too many people, myself partly included, spend most of their time and energy making money and don't take the time, or have the time, for enjoying nature. You're different, always seeking an intimate relationship with the wilds. I like your style, Tyler. You're getting both physical health and spiritual wealth," she said, playing it up for the kids.

She winked at Tyler, adding, "I know your rewards will be great as you continue searching for the secrets of the canyons."

Tyler explained further, "I love seeing and being amongst intensely beautiful scenes: crystal clear air, deep canyons, mountain peaks and valleys intertwining forever in the distance. It's amazing to explore among spectacular plants, rocks, and caves, to go underwater, and to view healthy natural environments."

Sierra broke in, "And you don't seem to mind a lot of hard work on the trail."

"That's right, and the tough physical effort required to really see it keeps us 'living.' Something motivates me in this direction," Tyler said. "It's the drummer I hear the beat of – my fate, or whatever you want to call it. Money might seem necessary, but it doesn't feed the soul. Now, if you can make money but not lose sight of the things that, as we say, feed the soul, then I suppose you've got it made."

Sierra sighed. "Yeah, you need a balance. It just comes down to what you do with the time that's given to you."

The two old friends continued philosophizing about how different people choose to lead their lives. Tyler struggled to rearrange his daypack head rest before settling back.

"There'll be no tame life for you, Tyler," Sierra concluded. "You like it wild, and that's what you'll get."

Tyler glanced up at the cave roof, wondering what would have happened if Sierra hadn't come; was he living too dangerously? Then he remembered how he felt like a glorious wild animal while venturing through untracked lands, climbing hand-over-hand up rock, or feeling his leg muscles burn as he summited lofty peaks. It may be risky, but it was his destiny. In addition, he wanted to share this exhilaration with others. For Tyler, wilderness adventure seemed like sunshine on a closed flower bursting into full bloom. When he found himself inside for too long, his soul appeared to wilt.

While Tyler's thoughts wandered, the conversation of the three Warriors lying comfortably together on the floor had taken a different turn.

"It would have been fun to live with the natural world like the Native Americans," said Shawnee. "My mom says we have some Aztec Indian blood, but mainly Spanish in my ancestry, so I'm considered Mexican."

"That's cool," said Makoa. "I'm an Island Native, mostly Hawaiian, and we have a little Samoan in us."

"You're from the far ocean cultures," said Colter. "That's awesome."

"But we left our tropical island home to come to the canyons of Arizona," Makoa went on. "What a switch. When I saw a show of the Grand Canyon and pictures taken from outer space of the canyon regions from Utah to northern Mexico, I didn't mind moving. They say it's one of the largest areas of canyons in the world."

“Well, I’m from the Great White North,” chuckled Colter. “Our family is Norwegian, and some Vikings appear in our family tree.”

"And don't forget that all of our common ancestors are believed to have come originally from Africa," said Sierra.

"How long will it take us to become Explorers?" Colter spoke up, changing the subject. He was always eager to conquer challenges; his strong will and determination matched his powerful build.

"We need experience, gained through adventures in different environments," said Makoa, "like the jungle, the ocean, and high snow-covered peaks."

"We've been caving," said Shawnee optimistically.

"It'll take forever," said Colter, "but I'm going to do it."

"Yeah, me too," said Makoa as Shawnee nodded in agreement.

"We'll all be Explorers," insisted Shawnee, "and even Eagle Chiefs one of these days, if we make the effort. It’s not easy."

Tyler had designated levels for his hikers to achieve. He called the youngest hikers, the four- to ten-year-olds, who were new to the wilderness, Braves. After a couple of years of experience and many age-appropriate adventures, they would have either found or been given a pair of antlers and become Bucks. At this level, the youths must know the basics of hiking and climbing, be able to recognize danger (such as loose rocks), appreciate scenic views and natural wonders, and act responsibly in the wilderness, including keeping a clean, safe camp.

Bucks who continued to gain experience from many trips and adventures became Pathfinders. Pathfinders possessed enough knowledge of the outdoors and the experience and instincts to find the best routes in the wilderness, with safety a critical concern.

As they grew up, those with the physical strength, courage, and knowledge to handle situations alone in almost any outdoor adventure achieved the title of Warriors. Warriors who explored many types of wilderness environments over extended periods of time, such as river running, mountain climbing, caving, underwater diving, backcountry skiing, sailing, and hiking became Explorers: adventurers with a craving for unexplored wonderlands.

One could finally become an Eagle Chief after years of exploring. At this level, an individual had to be an extremely knowledgeable adventurer with a great deal of experience and reliable judgment in a variety of outdoor situations and environments. Eagle Chiefs are naturalists with a deep love and respect for nature, and they are amateur scientists in many areas. Because of their experience with and spiritual connection to the natural world, they seem to have a sixth sense enabling them to read nature's signs while exploring the wilds.

Tyler was an Eagle Chief. Colter, Makoa, and Shawnee, all between fourteen and fifteen years old, had been exploring with Tyler since they were very young and were his youngest protégés ever to become Warriors. All were trusted friends.

From early boyhood, Makoa loved nature and wild creatures, had kept many animals, and spent almost all his free time and attention on these two interests. From the time spent alone caring for his pets or wandering the open country around his house, he acquired the skills of an observer and thinker. His personality was gentle, steady, quiet, and calm, so being around him was a peaceful experience.

Though, like all young people, he could still be full of fun. His spirit ran deep with a blaze of passion for the natural world. He observed and learned from interesting scenes or events in nature, often sitting for minutes at a time with his emerald-green eyes wide and still.

Ever since Makoa was a small boy, Tyler, who also loved wild animals, had encouraged him in this field. The two of them trained a red-tailed hawk for falconry, and Tyler helped Makoa build a snake pit and turtle pond behind his house. Makoa also kept saltwater aquariums, an eight-foot boa, an armadillo, a tamed spotted skunk, a raccoon, and a parrot which he had taught to talk. He had already made up his mind to be a wildlife biologist or veterinarian. From high in the branches of his tree fort, Makoa's quest for adventure grew as he read tales of explorers and the wild lands and animals they came across. His other love was swimming, and it seemed his island ancestry had granted him strength and fluidness in the water.

Colter's passion was sports. He played soccer, baseball, basketball, and football. He excelled at these games at a competitive level, and not only because of his physical prowess; he had learned, with Tyler's help, to tap into his inner strength and to keep his constantly rambling mind on a positive track.

Colter had learned to heighten his awareness in competition. His bright blue eyes became a blank glare, picking up everything, and he could unleash a focused thunderbolt of energy – sure, swift, and strong – at the necessary moment of action. He controlled his mind by keeping it busy with creative thoughts so that negative ones would not propagate. He might do this by imagining he was a mountain lion or eagle, or simply by concentrating on his breath or any other single act. Either technique would keep his mind from wandering into negative territory. With these mental skills honed, he became an iron-willed machine during games, would not choke, and was able to "peak" or "zone" at just the right moment.

Tyler encouraged Colter to think positively and taught him to trust and have faith in himself and his abilities. As his role model, Tyler told him that for these skills to be successful at higher levels, he would need to build the adequate strength, put in the practice, and let time provide the experience.

Above all, the boy learned to respect his opponents and foster better feelings in the heat of battle, to love life and not hate his adversaries. This allowed him to relax, which he always remembered to do to keep his movements fluid. His interaction with nature and the outdoors provided tranquility, and the lack of competition gave him a mental break from sports.

At the same time, the many energetic wilderness adventures greatly increased his strength. His friends and teammates felt that with all his gifts, Colter's best attribute was his kindness and caring toward others.

Shawnee also identified as an athlete whose main interest besides adventuring was horseback riding. She liked to jump and barrel race, and she had been competing in horse shows and rodeos since her childhood. On the back of a horse, she became one with the animal. The reins served as telegraph wires, keeping the minds of horse and rider in constant communication, although mostly her legs and body gave the subtle signals to direct her horse around or over obstacles.

Shawnee also had a keen interest in and appreciation of the wilderness, thanks in large part to Tyler. She had hiked with his group for years, acquiring a love of the wild through many experiences and gaining an understanding of both the hardships and rewards that often resulted from their undertakings. She had been forged well for this life, tempered slowly like the strongest steel.

Even though the three Warriors behaved quite differently in many respects, they all shared a love of nature and the wilderness. Tyler started hiking with each of them at different times between the ages of five and eight, and their unique personalities brought much joy to his life.

Tyler made a living by guiding people on hikes through the mountains and canyons surrounding Tucson, Arizona, his home. Throughout the week, he led adults from the various resorts and hotels in town and occasionally youth groups. But on weekends, Tyler hiked and explored with friends, both young and old. Many a young child he had raised on the trails in the past thirty years, and even as adults, some continued exploring with him. Now he also helped to introduce their children to the great outdoors.

After a while, their candlelight conversations wound down, and all promised once again to keep the mummy cave a closely guarded secret. Being tried and trusted friends, they felt confident that news of their find would not irresponsibly escape through any one of them. Soon fast asleep, their heads filled with dreams of wondrous lost Indian treasures. Tyler's dreams took an added twist as he went flying, endlessly searching for something, winding through canyons with emerald-green plants, high red cliffs, towering white waterfalls, and beautiful clear-blue rivers. And so the night passed.

When everyone awoke, they felt they had been far away and just returned from a long but peaceful journey. In the dark, quiet cave, having slept deeply, each of the Warriors felt amazingly well-rested and satisfied. The youngsters realized they had lived their dreams the day before when discovering the mummy cave. Little did they know of the real journey awaiting them.

While the adventurers packed their belongings and removed all traces of their visit to the cave, including the candle wax, Tyler sketched the eagle petroglyph. He took care to duplicate each line and the precise location of the arrowhead. Then they climbed out of the burial chamber using their tough yucca rope. Once outside, everyone helped to gather large quantities of brush and dead wood to hide the entrance. Finally satisfied that the camouflage looked natural and that no one could see the mouth of the cave, Tyler, Sierra, and the Warriors headed down the mountain. Beau again led the way.

Kids and Falls

Ben Metcalf

2

The Old Pueblo

The mountains look like Indians facing up to the sky.
As we watch with wonder through silhouettes of cacti,
A hawk flies into the desert sunset to its nest,
And mountains turn deep purple off toward the west.
Around the fire we play our song to the night.
Mysteries of the Hohokam . . .
Would the petroglyph shed light?

After coming down from the Hohokam mummy cave, the Warriors went back to their comfortable casas in Tucson, often called the Old Pueblo. It was a fairly small city then and not what one might expect of a so-called "desert" town. Mountains nearly 10,000 feet in height rose on two sides of the valley like towering castles, their granite buttresses clearly visible from anywhere in the city. To the south a bit farther is a third giant mountain. The streams and rugged canyons that cut through these peaks are a powerful lure to the hardy souls who seek out adventure and the secret spots.

This Arizona country holds a great variety of landscapes: rock walled canyons with cactus-hung cliffs and deep pools, leading up to forests of giant ponderosa pines and Douglas firs. There's something for every season.

Tyler lived in a 100-year-old adobe on the edge of Tucson, surrounded by natural desert. His friends called his house "the museum" because it contained many interesting natural objects that Tyler collected on his journeys. An incredible botanical garden surrounded the house with cacti of all shapes and sizes scattered among the desert trees and creosote bushes. Tyler had spent years growing different species of cactus, not only from Arizona, but also from many other parts of the world.

Winding trails went past the odd totem pole cacti, walls of giant prickly pear, Joshua trees, and all sorts of fancifully shaped foliage. Maintaining this wild garden of thickly packed plants was his hobby, keeping him busy while at home.

Over time, some of the cacti had grown to enormous sizes and produced numerous babies for transplanting. Tree-climbing cacti and vines wove their way up and onto ramadas, built with wood gathered from the desert: forked mesquite trunks for the posts, dried wooden interior "ribs" of the giant saguaro cacti for the roof, and saguaro "boots" for decoration.

These boot-like objects were the old holes of Gila woodpecker and gilded flicker nests, dried hard like cardboard and left after most of the cactus had rotted away.

Tyler's yard had become a sanctuary to many wild desert animals. Several varieties of lizards visited in the late spring, summer, and early fall months, including horned lizards, zebra tails, leopard lizards, Gila monsters, and turquoise collared lizards. Snakes also passed through the property. His favorite, the Arizona king snake boasted a bold black coloring with thin white stripes. This favored reptile included in its diet other snakes and could hopefully chase off any rattlers that happened by.

His king snake lived in the garden, but occasionally a rattler might be found sunning on the porch. Because rattlers are so territorial, Tyler would have no choice but to catch the intruder with a snake stick, put it in a pillowcase, and release it far enough away that it wouldn't come back. He generally drove for many miles before releasing the rattler where it would have to make do with a new home and, he hoped, survive against the odds.

Tyler never tired of observing with satisfaction the great variety of wildlife. Javelinas, coyotes, deer, and bobcats came near the house, and every once in a while, he spotted a mountain lion track.

He loved watching the lizards chasing each other around the desert, doing their pushups or climbing trees. He also looked forward to seeing the huge, homely Colorado River toads that showed up on summer evenings after the rains and tried to catch bugs, like the giant black paloverde beetles attracted by the porch light.

When Tyler returned from the trip to the mummy cave, he could not wait to go to his dad's house and tell him what they had found. After explaining everything seen in the cave, his father said he would write up a report to the forest service and attempt to find support and funding for a way to survey and protect the precious site.

After this meeting, Tyler went home to sit in the garden with Beau and relax in the afternoon sun. This year's early spring season had come with good rains, and bright green grass grew everywhere, making the desert especially beautiful. The next day, Monday, he planned to stay home and improve his garden by moving a few cacti. On Tuesday he would be leading a school group on a hike up a local canyon, and throughout the rest of the week, he had resort customers to guide.

He wandered through his garden as the resident curve-billed thrasher shrieked a greeting. Many desert birds served as daily companions for him at home.

Among the avian visitors were brilliantly colored hummingbirds, roadrunners, bright red cardinals, and peaceful doves with their soft calls carrying out over the desert. Arizona's state bird, the fearless cactus wren, often came onto Tyler's porch searching for bugs. A fair number of hawks passed through, including the large Red-tailed variety, Harris hawks, and the smaller bird hunters such as Cooper's, Sharp-shinned, and Goshawks. In the evenings, Tyler loved the company of little screech owls that perched on the porch, and the elf owls, smallest of all owls, could often be heard making their faint calls in the desert. Large great horned owls visited too but usually stayed higher up, on top of the saguaros or trees.

The same thrasher continued calling incessantly from the top of a saguaro skeleton as Tyler went inside to unpack. He took the rolled-up tracing of the eagle petroglyph and stored it in a drawer for safekeeping, wondering as he put it away whether it really constituted a map, or had his imagination gotten the best of him this time. Dismissing it from his mind and knowing he could make time tomorrow to study the sketch thoroughly, he fed Beau, then himself, and went to bed exhausted.

As the next day dawned, Tyler swung open the large wooden door of his bedroom and stretched in the warmth of the rising sun. He stepped onto the east-facing porch built with hand-cut log beams and framed with saguaro ribs and gazed out upon a peaceful scene. Beau bounded out with him. It was another spring morning without a cloud in the sky; the distant mountains appeared clear and close, rising into the infinite blue.

While enjoying the morning shadows and the strange forms of the different cacti, Tyler thought about the mummy cave, then began to work before the sun rose any higher. His wanderlust felt satisfied for the moment, and he intended to get some plants into the ground.

He cut some sections earlier from a few large prickly pear and organ pipe cacti growing into the trail. Their cut ends had dried with a scab-like skin and now looked ready to be planted. He also reserved some new, tender prickly pear cactus pads to be cooked and eaten later.

He set to work expanding his exotic garden while Beau slept in the sun. Spotting a large spiny lizard on a beam in the ramada, Tyler went into the house for a container of mealworms bought from the pet store. He threw some on the ground where the lizard could see them, and right away the big spiny came down to eat. Tyler had always fed the lizards, and many turned out to be quite tame. Before long, this spiny stood on his shoe, eating worms from his hand.

At the end of the week, Tyler was working into the afternoon, digging and planting, contentedly creating his bit of paradise. The sun felt good, but occasionally he would rest in the shade of a ramada. Toward the end of the day, he heard voices down the long dirt driveway. Running to the back porch, he grabbed a saguaro rib "spear," glided silently to the side of the house, and hid behind a thick patch of prickly pear.

Peeking through the plants, he spotted the Warriors, Shawnee, Colter, and Makoa, walking around a bend in the driveway. They were being dropped off for the evening while their parents had company parties or adult gatherings to attend.

Tyler gave a war whoop, and seeing that they all looked his way, let the "spear" fly in a high lobbing arc, aimed off to the side. Colter jumped out, his long, bright-blond hair shining in the sun, and caught it as it came down. Hardly knowing his own strength, he threw it straight back to Tyler, who had to leap out of the way. Beau ran to the Warriors, enthusiastically making the rounds and getting rewarded by eager pats of love and acceptance.

While the group walked toward a ramada to sit and visit, Colter spoke up. "My parents said thanks for having us over for a barbecue."

"What's been going on?" Tyler asked. "Grab a log to sit on. Glad you could come help."

"I've been riding my horse," answered Shawnee, "and started helping mentally and physically challenged children ride at the stable."

"What's that like?" asked Makoa.

"It's really interesting! These kids seem to appreciate the smallest things. Seeing their incredible joy when riding made me realize what an amazing opportunity it is. I have so much more fun when I ride now."

"You're both giving something to each other," said Tyler. "I hope you stick with it; it's a nice feeling to help others."

"I'm going to. I really love it, and so do the kids."

"Good for you, Shawnee." Then Tyler turned to Makoa and said, "Do you still have that tokay gecko loose in your room?"

"Yeah, I do," said Makoa, chuckling. He looked at the others and giggled. "Last week when Tyler came over for dinner, he went to turn a light on, and the gecko bit him. He was sitting right on the switch! I about died laughing when you screamed."

"Yeah, you'd yell, too," Tyler said. "I've got to watch it when I go to your house. You never know what critter might jump on you. Hey, you guys want to help me move a five-foot saguaro?"

"Sure," they answered.

"Let's go get it; I've had it on the porch in the shade for about two weeks now, letting the root dry so it won't rot. I got it from the back of the property where it was falling off a wash bank." Tyler reminded his friends, "Unless on private property, a permit is needed to transport a saguaro. They are illegal to take from the wild. Let's mark the south-facing side to make sure it faces the same way when replanted."

If another side was exposed to the hot southern sun, it would likely get sunburned and scarred. They put a rope around the thorny top part and lifted as Tyler carried the root, and off they went to plant the saguaro.

"Did you figure out if the eagle petroglyph is a map?" Makoa asked.

"I haven't studied it yet," Tyler said. "Maybe we'll look at it later."

While Tyler packed the dirt in the hole, the kids went into the house and brought out bows and arrows, hatchets, knives, and spears for a little primitive sports competition, mountain-man skills, as Tyler called it. He had set up a hay bale for the arrows and spear and a thick throwing post for the hatchet and knife.

The Warriors, following strict safety procedures, started practicing and soon challenging one another to contests as Tyler watched.

Colter showed his strong, natural throwing motion with the hatchet and spear from his years of sports, while Makoa excelled in the knife throw with his deft touch. Shawnee's positive, steady way made her a champion of the bow and arrow. Tyler joined them before long, always enjoying a good contest, and with years of practice behind him, amazed his friends with accuracy and consistency.

"Let's get the barbecue going," Tyler suddenly announced.

The Warriors worked on building a fire at one of the ramadas using mesquite wood, since its smoke gives meat a great flavor. The sun began to set, highlighting the stickery silhouettes of the Joshua trees, saguaros, and yuccas with a backdrop of brilliant gold turning to blazing red and orange.

Tyler and his friends climbed a large wooden pueblo-style ladder to the top of the house for a better view and stared in appreciation. A pair of nighthawks, relatives of the whip-poor-will, chased each other around the desert, gliding with quick turns through the scene.

The last rays from the sun lit up the many giant saguaros on the nearby hills, casting a shadow behind each one. The suggested movement made them look like an army marching down on the city.

The silhouette of mountains jutting up on the western side of the desert basin turned a shade of dark purple, their jagged outlines appearing like the profiles of giant Indians gazing up to the sky. Across the valley floor, the lights of Tucson glittered like gold dust. For the Warriors, not all the treasures of life were hidden in a secret cave.

While his young friends enjoyed the sunset, Tyler placed the meat and vegetables on the grill to slowly cook over the hot mesquite coals. The kids carefully climbed down from the roof, went into the house, and came out with musical instruments. Makoa handed Tyler his bag of harmonicas, and everyone settled around the fire. The music immediately began to flow. Shawnee and Colter strummed a steady rhythm on their guitars, and Makoa soon joined in with the fiddle, taking turns playing the lead with Tyler, who wailed on his harmonica.

Sierra appeared out of nowhere, having driven up without their hearing, and sat down beside the conga drum, maracas, and tambourines, quickly getting into the rhythm. Their instruments blended and intertwined like currents in a stream as they dispatched this high-energy music into the utterly still desert night. They played without stopping, simply letting their feel for the music guide them.

Now and again, Tyler checked on the food, or one of the Warriors took a break and walked off to listen and gaze back at the fire and the giant desert plants glowing in its light. After a half-hour of continuous music, everyone put the instruments down, helped to serve dinner, and sat back and talked around the smoldering embers.

"Tyler, why do you love the wilderness so much?" Shawnee asked.

Colter threw a stick into the fire, and it blazed up instantly, casting a bright light on Tyler. The Warriors stared at their friend and teacher, lit up as if on stage. Like the mountain men and Indians of the past, he kept his hair a little long. His legs, gnarled and muscular, provided him with the agility of a tennis player; his shoulders were broad like a surfer's, and his corded-steel forearms hung loose, suggesting lightning reflexes. With so much time spent in the wild under "free" skies, Tyler had a rugged look, like he'd been dipped in tannin.

Tyler cocked his head like a bird to consider the question. As the fire illuminated his brilliant blue-green eyes, he answered with a thoughtful speech, "I love the wilderness – its incomparable beauty landscaped with Nature's superior 'eye,' incredible gardens of wild plants, and amazing rock formations.

"The lives of the animals that weave their way through these wonderlands and the secrets of nature are inexhaustible and infinitely interesting. When I go to the canyons or any wilderness area, I search for a beautiful, peaceful spot, usually far from people. On any hike there is always the possibility of discovering something exciting, new, or beautiful. There's usually enough time to feel unhurried and to see things clearly, especially oneself."

"When I get to a spot deemed worthy, I might sit on a rock by a rushing stream or wherever the view is good, and simply take in the power and peace of the hills. I don't do much but observe the beauty and life around me. I might lie back and watch a cloud grow. Sometimes there's no thought, as though I'm just a conscious part of nature; I just am. The wilderness makes me tranquil, gives me strength and health, as well as peace of mind. Great joy comes from a beautiful time spent in the wilds, whether sitting, walking, climbing, swimming, caving, skiing, sailing, or whatever. This feeling surpasses almost any other we can experience on Earth, except for the arts and love. You might say nature never lets me down. It purifies my soul and restores it with peace."

"That was a mouthful," teased Sierra, "and well said."

"I hope there are always great areas of wilderness to experience and explore, without too many people," threw in Makoa.

"Wilderness," Shawnee said aloud to herself. "The sound of the word itself is enchanting."

"I agree," said Tyler. "It creates a picture of dramatically beautiful, untamed lands, lots of animals, pure water, and clean air. Native Americans of the past saw the wilderness as a place where great beauty and peace reign, a paradise providing everything they needed. The first rugged mountain men who left their homes in the east to move out west also shared this love and view of the wilderness. But some people who came afterward, many of them having lived too long in the cities, had the attitude that the wilderness was hostile and needed to be conquered, tamed, or pushed back so 'civilization' could get a foothold."

The kids huddled closer to the fire as Sierra took up the conversation so that Tyler could eat.

"Things have started to change," she went on. "In this environmentally aware age, people are adopting another view of nature, seeing it as much more fragile than in the old days. Nature and wilderness used to be seen as limitless, so vast that humans could hardly make a dent.

Now we know nature can no longer protect herself against us. We must protect her from ourselves."

Sierra knew what she was talking about. "You know, I work as a sustainability strategist. I try to help companies choose materials for their products that are sustainable by the planet and will either biodegrade harmlessly or be recycled. People all around the world are finally learning the lesson that the Native Americans taught; nature must be protected, conserved, and held in great respect. Humans are part of the great web of life, and whatever happens to that web affects every living thing. In other words, in nature, small changes can lead to a cascade of other changes."

"It's not just Native Americans," said Makoa. "Most of the Native people of the world live, or lived, in harmony with nature. The pygmies of the African Congo call the rainforest their mother because it takes care of them, giving them what's needed to survive. They often 'tattoo' themselves with charcoal from their forest's trees to remind themselves of this and to show their connection to, and respect for, their natural world.

Sierra lamented, "I don't think the world can really stand to lose any more rich, natural areas. We should fight tooth and nail to save them."

"I couldn't stand to live without wilderness," said Colter. "Especially after all the adventures we've had and all the beauty and wildlife we've seen."

"Me neither," said Makoa. "These memories will probably be some of the greatest of our lives."

"There may still be time left to save the Earth and lots of special places," said Shawnee. "I hope so, anyway."

"I also hope humans can achieve a sustainable population for the world," Tyler said, "and people like Sierra continue to work on solutions for sustainable products."

"It's about time people looked at wild, natural areas as many Native people living close to the land have historically. We have to do whatever we can to save the earth from environmental catastrophe," added Sierra.

Their conversation slowed as the "dreamers" gazed beyond the fire ring to the cacti and trees illuminated by the flickering flames. Being surrounded in this way by the beauty and power of nature gave them a strong sense of hope.

Tyler and Sierra went for a walk around the garden. Colter searched for more firewood while Shawnee and Makoa had a conversation of their own.

"Your parents like for you to go on hikes and adventures, don't they?" asked Shawnee. "Even though there could be risks?"

"Yeah," Makoa replied. "They think it's healthy for me to be outdoors, especially with other kids who love it. They know risks are everywhere."

Shawnee sighed. "My parents like nature, but they're not into wilderness adventures. Sometimes they have a hard time letting me go; they're fairly protective. Dad appreciates my sense of adventure and love of nature and wants me to be strong, and whenever I'm really passionate about doing something or going somewhere, Mom usually lets me."

"That's cool," said Makoa. "I guess we're both pretty lucky. We're able to do what we love; not everybody gets the chance."

Tyler and Sierra had taken their seats once again around the fire, stirring and poking at the coals. A stream of sparks rose as if from a volcano.

Tyler spoke up, "Hey, Makoa, are we going to release the hawk this weekend?" Tyler, a General Falconer, had spent the last two years training a red-tailed hawk, and Makoa often helped him.

"Yeah, let's do it," answered Makoa. "It's time for him to be free."

Starting to put her percussion instruments away, Sierra turned to the group and said, "That's your adventure, but let me know when you do. I want to watch." After giving Tyler a quick hug, she said,

"Adios! See you all soon," and headed back to her car. Tyler walked her out.

When Tyler came back, the Warriors resumed their conversation.

"Isn't Coonie also about ready to take off on his own?" asked Makoa, referring to Tyler's pet raccoon.

"I know," answered Tyler. "He's getting pretty independent...and moody. He nipped me really hard the other day. I'm going to miss taking him on hikes."

It was now obvious that Coonie wanted to be free and travel by his own lights. Tyler had crafted a large enclosure for the animal around the trunk of a big mesquite tree near the house, but now Coonie needed to explore and live in the wild.

"Let's release him down in the cottonwood trees on the Tanque Verde," said Tyler, stirring the coals around unburned wood. "But we'll talk about that later. It's getting late. Guess we better pack it up."

After putting everything away, Tyler asked the Warriors to have a look at the tracing of the mummy-cave petroglyph. Taking it from the drawer, he laid it on the large mesquite-burl table in the living room. A small gecko high on the wall seemed to be eavesdropping.

"My hope," Tyler began, "is that this is a secret map. These cracks among the feathers on the eagle's chest could represent canyons, rivers, and streams. Like we were thinking before, this arrowhead might be marking something important like a turquoise mine or special clay bank of hematite – who knows.

"It may even have been a ritualistic hunting symbol, the hunter asking for his arrow to be guided with the swiftness and eyes of the eagle.

"Hang on a second," he interrupted himself. Like a giant spider, he used the windowsill to climb up and retrieve his Arizona relief map from the top of the bookcase. Dropping back to the floor without any wasted motion, he laid the map next to the tracing. The Warriors gathered around, looking on as Tyler searched the different sections of the state trying to find a pattern of river lines or canyons that matched the petroglyph map. His hand extended like a hooded cobra over its prey as he gestured above one map and then the other. Soon they were all bent over the maps with their fingers tracing the many waterways.

"Look at this!" Tyler finally said, pointing somewhat in disbelief. "Doesn't this river look like the main line or crack on the petroglyph? Here's where it branches off." His heart flinched. Sure enough, the lines of the petroglyph matched the rivers and streams crisscrossing an area in the east-central part of the state.

"Can it be a coincidence?" questioned Shawnee.

"Let's see where the arrowhead sits," said Tyler, leaning back over the map. "Look! Its placement corresponds to this smaller creek flowing into the main stream, and you all know these canyons. It's not that far of a walk from the mummy cave, about two days is all. It's a possibility."

The Warriors stared at the map, wondering what sort of adventures might arise next.

"The arrowhead is marked on the creek where the emerald pool is!" Tyler said excitedly. "We should take a trip in a couple of weeks and check it out. You all have spring break then with two weeks off school, right? Maybe your parents will let you go."

"Yeah, almost two and a half," said Shawnee. "Hey, we can stop by my aunt and uncle's ranch. They've got new goats."

"We usually do," responded Tyler.

The Warriors were always eager for adventure like an arrow is for flight as it trembles on the string, The excitement showed plainly on their faces.

Tyler marked the place on the map indicated by the arrowhead. Then he and the Warriors made initial plans for the weekend camping trip, looking ahead and wondering about what the exceptionally beautiful canyon might reveal this time.

To conclude the night, Tyler and the kids walked back out into the still desert. A pack of coyotes howled their age-old song as the adventurers, surrounded by giant cacti, gazed up at the bright constellation of Orion the Hunter. Tyler liked to call this winter constellation the "Warrior" and habitually pointed it out to his protégés. Soon his Warriors, one by one, said good-bye as their parents arrived to take them home.

Tyler headed off to bed. Wild thoughts of where the "map" might lead raced through his mind. Knowing he needed plenty of rest for the youth group he would be guiding tomorrow, he made himself relax and soon fell asleep.

That Sunday, he paid his dad another visit. His father's network of archeologists had not been notified of Tyler's mummy cave yet, since a preliminary plan was being written up. This discovery intrigued Tyler's father enough to bring him back from retirement. When he showed his dad the petroglyph alongside the Arizona relief map, Dr. Young expressed excitement for this new quest, but doubted that much would come of it.

Jaguar
Marc B. Wilson

3

Jaguar Canyon

The Earth, where man sprouted, is his home.
Nourished by this environment,
humans have flourished.
This beautiful blue planet is very rare,
maybe the only one that offers so much
to us. The variety of life and
landscapes are, as we know, unbelievable.
I hope man can cherish and protect the earth,
and keep from polluting and overpopulating it.
That is my greatest hope.

By the time spring break rolled around, Tyler was packed and ready for the three-day trip. Early on Saturday morning, the Warriors' parents dropped their hearty adventurers off at his house. Everyone felt eager for the hike up the secluded canyon shown on the petroglyph.

They brought sleeping bags, water bottles, ground sheets, small flashlights, backpacks, and a bare minimum of clothes and personal equipment. The forecast predicted high temperatures in the 80s and lows in the 50s, perfect spring camping weather. Each hiker wore sturdy sandals or old tennis shoes since they anticipated crossing or walking in the stream often. A swim in the beautiful emerald pool would also be hard to resist.

By midmorning, they headed off in Tyler's one-ton van with its custom saguaro-ribbed interior roof. It would take a couple of hours to get to the wilderness canyon deep in the Galiuro Mountains. For extra safety on this trip, Tyler brought an emergency locator device. It could connect to a satellite and only needed a view of the sky to work; with the press of a button, the most reasonable means of recue would be initiated.

After crossing several desert valleys surrounded by tall, ragged mountains, Tyler turned off on a dirt road leading toward the distant canyon.

Along the way they admired thick stands of saguaro, ocotillo, cholla cacti, and carpets of spring flowers: dark-pink owl clover, white chicory, blue lupine, and orange poppies. The flowers grew thicker until finally the group couldn't resist the temptation to take a short break.

" Javelinas!" shouted Makoa, pointing. On a nearby slope, a group of the wild boar-like animals quickly moved out of view.

"We always see lots of animals in this canyon," Makoa said. "I wonder what we'll see this time."

"I hope we find another Indian cave," Tyler wished.

After photographing some of the wildflowers, they hopped back in the van. The Warriors instinctively looked for Beau to come running behind, but in this canyon, a protected wilderness with a bighorn sheep herd and many other wild animals, no dogs were allowed. Beau had been left at home with Sierra.

The road went along the perennial creek flowing through a lush riparian forest. Huge cottonwoods, smooth, white-barked sycamores, Arizona ash, desert hackberry, Arizona black walnut, mesquite, and desert willows all stood nestled at the bottom of rugged rock cliffs and cactus-strewn hills. A few isolated ranches hugged the higher banks where the land was flatter and out of reach of floods.

"There's my aunt and uncle's ranch. Can we stop in and see the new goats?" asked Shawnee.

"No, not right now," Tyler said. "We'd be there for hours. We'll have time on the way back. I asked your mom to call them and tell 'em we'd try to stop on the way home."

Eventually the road ended. After making final preparations with Tyler equally distributing the food, they shouldered their packs and headed up the creek into the deepening canyon. Flanked by green stream-side vegetation, they kept close to the water, crossing it many times. The surrounding hills farther from the water were thick with plants that preferred the drier zone: saguaros, creosote, jojoba, cholla, and palo verdes. Green grasses spread everywhere from the winter rains, and turquoise lichen and bright green moss colored the cliffs farther up the canyon.

Suddenly, a Harris hawk flew in front of them as it chased a quail, and then two more came in from the side. One hawk swiftly struck its prey, and a shower of feathers fell to the ground.

"Wow!" said Colter. "That was amazing."

"Stay still so they'll have a chance to eat it," said Tyler. Just then, one of the hawks dropped down, grabbed the dead quail, and flew off in the direction of its hunting partners. Harris hawks hunt in packs, a unique strategy among birds of prey. While the Warriors hiked on through the shallow water, they delighted in herding fish: small schools of spike-dace, loach minnows, and Sonoran suckers. This had become not only a habit of theirs, but a favorite pastime in the canyon for kids in general.

Towering cliffs began to appear along the creek. As a large shadow crossed their path, the group looked up to see a common black hawk landing on a dead snag protruding from the rock face. It screeched, took off, then soared overhead. They could see the hawk's white-striped tail and incredible broad wings.

"Its nest is probably nearby," said Tyler. After a brief scan of their surroundings, he motioned, "There, at the top of that big cottonwood."

They hiked along below the cliffs through a forest of desert hackberry, an African-looking tree with gray bark, bright green leaves, and elephant-like "eyes" that seemed to wink at them. As they maneuvered around giant boulders strewn across this part of the canyon, Shawnee announced the presence of crystals embedded in pockets within the bedrock.

Brightly colored birds flashed through the thickets and trees: yellow warblers, vermillion flycatchers, and red and yellow tanagers.

“Guys, listen – a summer tanager,” Colter stated upon recognizing a whistling and chattering in the treetops. The young Warriors knew the birds of the area.

Farther up the narrowing canyon, a small waterfall tumbled down from a shallow side cleft in the wall. The tall cliffs enclosing the falls were terraced with moss-covered ledges exotically landscaped with saguaros of various sizes, barrel cacti, and impressive blue-green agaves. High above, vultures circled in groups or individually sailed across cliff faces, gliding like paper airplanes in and out of jagged rock spires.

"A bighorn!" Tyler excitedly announced, pointing to the highest cliffs. While he spoke, the large ram walked out onto a ledge overlooking the canyon. Large wreaths of prickly pear grew out of cracks in the ground around the animal. As the ram walked closer to the edge, he knocked off a dead section of cactus that came crashing down the 200-foot rock face, falling in pieces at their feet. The king of the canyons struck a majestic pose, surveying his rugged domain. The Warriors watched in awe until the ram sauntered out of view.

"Wow, he tried to ambush us," joked Tyler. "Let's keep going."

In the late afternoon, the Warriors and Tyler came across a beautiful spring flowing from a steep side canyon. They decided to make their first night's camp on a sandy beach where the spring ran into the main creek. Available at the head of the spring was pure water, filtered through the tons of earth above.

In this area, a lush paradise of tall, dark green ferns, bright yellow columbines, and red monkey flowers surrounded the group of friends. Large trees covered with grape vines provided welcome shade until the sun dropped behind the cliffs. The travelers would not reach the side canyon indicated by their petroglyph map until the following day.

"Let's hurry and set up camp so we'll have enough time to climb to the lookout," said Tyler. It was a favorite place of his to overlook the canyon. Makoa and Colter volunteered to collect firewood, and Shawnee started digging a firepit in the sand so their ashes could be easily covered later. Tyler got to work opening packs and setting out the cooking gear and sleeping bags. Once they had finished these tasks, they grabbed only water bottles and began to hike up the steep side canyon through a series of beautiful little pools.

"Check it out – a mud turtle," Makoa pointed out as it slipped from the bank, swimming off to hide. At the head of the spring, hidden behind a veil of ferns, water flowed out of the cliff wall. They filled all the water bottles, leaving a few there to pick up on the way back to camp. From here on up, the stream disappeared beneath boulders the size of cars or larger. Without their backpacks weighing them down, the youngsters enjoyed the freedom of the gymnastics-like workout, climbing through the giant rocks and up the cliffs.

Tyler reminded everyone, "Don't forget that the biggest danger in these mountains is loose, unstable rocks."

They all knew from experience that even the slightest pull could bring a boulder down on a careless climber, and a single misjudged step on a loose rock could send one flying into the dirt or off a cliff. Tyler guided them through the dangerous terrain with an experienced eye.

Topping out above a set of dry falls, they traversed out to a ledge for a good view of the sunset. Immediately after settling down on a large rock, bighorns were spotted under the higher cliffs. The group of ewes and lambs took off running along the ledges and over the boulders. The frisky, energetic lambs led the way, bouncing up steep rock walls to flat ledge tops and posing for a moment with heads all turned in the same direction before galloping off to new challenges. The herd moved steadily across a large natural amphitheater, keeping a wary eye on the Warriors. Reaching the far side, some sheep stopped to nibble on something while others stood as lookouts on rock pinnacles.

"I'd like to see you tame and ride a bighorn, Shawnee," Tyler joked.

"I'd sure like to," she said. "Look what strong climbers they are – unreal."

Relaxing on their rocky perch, the Warriors felt content and filled with a sense of peace as they looked through a stand of saguaro skeletons to a perfect view of the towering cliffs lining the tree-filled canyon below. Flocks of vultures circled above, preparing to roost in communal perches. A large dark bird flew over the rim. Close behind on either side, two lighter-colored birds followed.

Tyler clarified what they just witnessed together, "That's a golden eagle being chased by red-tails!".

The smaller hawks, more agile than the eagle, were chasing it out of their territory. When they came too close, the eagle rolled, showing its massive, curved talons. Then it lost the hawks by tucking its wings and shooting across the canyon in a steep-angled dive, ultimately disappearing behind a bend in the canyon wall. This final great sighting brought an end to a good day. Seeing such exhilarating scenery and wildlife left them deeply satisfied; what a lonely world it would be without natural beauty and our animal friends. The cliff shone brightly in the last rays of the setting sun.

As light faded to dusk, Tyler and the kids hiked back to camp, climbing carefully to avoid the many areas of unstable rock. While retracing their steps through the giant boulders, there echoed a sound like baby sheep "baaing."

The group knew it was just the singing of the Arizona canyon tree frogs. Jumping about like a band of raccoons, the Warriors stopped to catch and release a few of the frogs before heading down.

Once back at camp, they quickly got the fire going to boil water for dinner: a simple freeze-dried backpacker's meal with nuts and dried fruit for snacks. Nobody minded the "camp food" as long as it was seasoned with plenty of adventure and beautiful scenery.

Late that evening after everyone had gone to bed and the camp fell quiet, Tyler heard the rattle of a branch against a rock. He flicked on his flashlight and saw a cute fuzzy face with big, round eyes staring back at him. The ringtail cat, looking like a cross between a fox, raccoon, and cat with large eyes and ears, is Arizona's state mammal. They are great climbers, able to smoothly go up and down cliffs or trees. Tyler, catching this ringtail scouting around camp for food, woke everyone in time to see it run off. However, it soon returned, followed by another; both raced down a trunk using their small, sharp semi-retractable claws. Amazingly, a ringtail can rotate its back feet 180 degrees and descend a tree with the same control and agility as when ascending. The ringtails moved quickly and silently around camp, then ran off chasing and screeching at each other as the Warriors fell back to sleep.

Tyler looked up through the trees at the bright stars above and saw a meteor blaze across the sky between the cliffs before he, too, drifted off to sleep.

Early the next morning after a good night's sleep and a breakfast of oatmeal and hot chocolate, everyone packed and headed up the canyon. They hiked beneath a giant overhang with a perfect sand floor.

Tyler explained, "This is said to be where the Apache Kid was born. Although an Apache, he was a top scout for the U.S., but turned into a notorious renegade because of an unfortunate incident."

About midday, the travelers reached the side canyon that Tyler believed was the one marked on the eagle petroglyph. They stopped for lunch at the junction and sat under a huge sycamore in the deep, green grass.

"The creek is running clear, so the 'emerald pool' should be in good shape, and I don't see any recent tracks left by humans. Perhaps we will have it all to ourselves," said Tyler.

When he and the Warriors turned into the narrower side chasm, they left the sounds of the larger stream behind. They found no human tracks in the damp sand and mud along the small stream, but many hand-like prints were seen of some nocturnal animals: raccoons, ringtails, and skunks.

"Look at this giant track!" Shawnee yelled. The boys ran over, startled to see such huge bird tracks. "What are these from?" Shawnee asked.

"That's a great blue heron," said Tyler. "I often see a solitary one or two in the canyons. Time to start looking for caves; this is the canyon marked with the arrowhead."

Farther along the creek, their progress slowed due to a mass of boulders and thick brush that forced them to bushwhack through tangled growth and climb over several enormous rocks before the streambed cleared and the going got easier. The cliffs closed in, towering 500 feet above. Bright green ground cover fringed their bases where rock met the streambed.

"These are edible plants known as miner's lettuce," Tyler pointed out. "Let's collect some for a salad later. We can mix it with watercress from the stream."

The Warriors stopped to eat and pick the good-tasting round leaves. In this narrower canyon, only the occasional gnarled tree grew along the side. Colter climbed into a small mesquite. Little tree lizards ran for cover as he sat in the thick lower branches watching his friends graze on the lettuce. A clump of mistletoe beside him was flowering; the strong, sweet scent put him in a dreamy mood.

After finishing gathering and grazing on miner's lettuce, the group hiked farther up the narrow canyon, exploring all the caves they came across. Tyler had again taken the lead.

Suddenly, he let out a startled cry. He quickly crouched to examine the ground at his feet, and the Warriors rushed to his side. He kept them back with outspread arms, for there in the mud was a large, perfectly preserved paw print of a very large cat, presumed to be an enormous mountain lion.

The awestruck Warriors shuddered at the thought of sharing this narrow canyon with such a large predator, though they also overflowed with excitement, danger being, of course, a great spice of life. Continuing onward with increased stealth and hoping to catch a glimpse of the large cat, each of them picked up a walking stick as soon as possible and held it like a spear in readiness. They crept forward, checking the many small caves at the base of the canyon wall. Some were only shallow, but beautiful, depressions beneath overhangs with dripping springs and carpets of moss.

Little sign of the ancients revealed itself to the adventurers, except for a potential chipped rock or two. They spotted hundreds of caves high up on the canyon walls, but these proved mostly inaccessible, so the search consisted of scrambling up to the reachable ones. Realizing the impossibility of exploring all the caves in the canyon, Tyler felt their chances of finding the one indicated on the petroglyph map, if it even was a map, quickly vanishing.

"Look up there!" shouted Colter, pointing to a large, round, and impressive arch framing the bright blue sky. The canyon walls at that location had many rocky outcroppings dotted with fancifully shaped spires, statues, and skulls. Vultures and small hawks constantly soared by these high-up sculptures.

Tyler and the Warriors moved on slowly until they heard a rustle near the cliff wall. A band of coatis, also called coatimundi, emerged. Adults and juveniles rushed past, dozens of them jumping and crashing through the undergrowth before calming down. They climbed the trees leaning onto the cliffs and worked their way up to the rocks where they resumed the endless search for food. The coatis looked under wood and stones for invertebrates, small vertebrates, and tubers.

As the friends proceeded, the stream started to collect into large clear blue pools fed by many small waterfalls. The scenery, so beautiful to be almost magical, held them at each new sight.

"Check out these tracks!" Colter excitedly shouted. The others rushed over to stare at the huge depressions leading up a nearby bank. These cat tracks had deep holes about the size of a thick nail at the end of each toe pad.

"Those are the claw marks," said Tyler. "Look at the size of them! Cats usually walk with their claws retracted, extending them to grab prey or when climbing up areas like this bank."

"Do you still want to go on?" Colter asked nervously. "It's getting kind of late; maybe we should camp here."

"We've got an hour or so left of good exploring before sunset," said Tyler. "Let's keep going for a while anyway. I would love to see that giant lion and get farther up by the emerald pool. It's strange that the cat's tracks are flat and broad at the base, more like a..."

Interrupted by a thunderous rumbling off the rock walls ahead, he whispered emphatically, "Listen!" and led them quickly onward. Moving cautiously around the next bend and ducking behind some large boulders, they peered into a small box canyon from where the noise seemed to come.

The scene transfixed them. They had caught a deadly chase in progress, the same life-or-death struggle played out over and over since life began on planet Earth, only with different characters. In this case, one of the combatants used to be plentiful in southern Arizona but was now very rare.

"A jaguar!?" said Tyler in a strange, hushed voice.

The Warriors looked on in astonishment as the large cat raced after five full-grown bighorn rams. The bighorns ran frantically, kicking up small rocks while they dodged the cat. The sound of hooves in the gravel echoed through the canyon. The rams evaded the great spotted beast again and again but eventually ended up cornered. They had probably come down an age-old route that Tyler could see worn into the wall behind them. The lead bighorn seemed to be eyeing it now as a means of escape. However, the first few moves up this path seemed to require climbing up difficult rocks that would give the jaguar time to catch them.

Tyler noticed the tracks at his feet and figured the jaguar had made his ambush from behind these very boulders. The Warriors watched, mesmerized, unseen by the predator or its prey. Momentarily trapped under an overhang, the rams stopped running and gathered with their giant curled horns turned toward the attacker.

The jaguar emitted a nasty snarl, then stood still. With a blood-tingling growl, he inched forward. As the growling mass of fury walked from side to side, he reached out a paw to slash the air now and then, intensified the deep snarling, and tried to get up the courage to charge the sturdy rams. Unable to stand the tension any longer, the bighorns took off in another wild run, kicking rocks into the face of the pursuing cat and cutting from side to side, barely escaping the hunter's raking claws.

Each time the rams headed for the main canyon, their only other chance of escape, the jaguar headed them off. The rams repeatedly eluded his grasp, then gathered for protection and a brief rest under the overhang. The great cat's patience wore thin; he finally attempted a foolish charge, even though the rams stood ready to defend themselves. The jaguar rushed in, reared up on his hind legs, and clawed at the shoulder of one of the bighorns, trying to get his fangs fastened on its neck. The ram responded by momentarily lowering his great curled horns, then bringing them up with a violent, smashing blow under the jaguar's jaws. The cat's head flew back in a whiplash motion as another ram attacked from the side, butting the cat again in the head.

The first two bighorns continued to deal the impatient cat quite a beating when yet another one rammed him in the ribs with tremendous force, catapulting the spotted beast onto a jumble of jagged rocks and knocking him unconscious. The jaguar remained motionless.

One by one the bighorns climbed the tricky ledges and made their way out of the canyon.

Leaving the protection of the boulder, the Warriors walked slowly toward the dead-looking cat.

"He might be only knocked out," Tyler warned, but none of them could resist moving in for a closer look. Giant curved claws hung from one of the front paws that draped over a rock. "I knew those looked like jaguar tracks."

"Look," said Makoa. "There's blood dripping under him."

"Looks like he landed hard on that jagged rock," Tyler said, "and might have punctured his rib cage."

"He's still breathing!" said Makoa excitedly. "Look at how much blood there is. He must have a deep cut. If we don't help him, he'll bleed to death."

Tyler decided right then and there he had to help the jaguar. Some sixth sense gave him confidence that the great beast wouldn't hurt him if he was careful. He reached beneath the huge cat and quickly found the large, deep puncture produced by the razor-edged pointed rock. Blood dripped freely from the wound as the cat lay unconscious.

Tyler called the Warriors over to help move the jaguar off the rocks. It took all their strength to roll, push, and drag him to a flat patch of sand mostly sheltered by a large overhanging boulder. They turned him so that the wound faced upward, and Tyler took some sterilized gauze pads from his first aid kit and laid them on the wound. Then he took off his shirt, washed it in the creek, and used it to apply pressure to stop the bleeding.

"He might also have a concussion and a broken rib or two," he said, leaning over the cat.

"Yeah, those first two rams gave his head a pretty good jolt," said Makoa. "What do you think we should do?"

"Well," said Tyler, unsure. "It looks like we should just camp here and keep an eye on him. We'll hunt for the cave later. We've got to think about this."

"What if he wakes up and attacks us?" asked Shawnee nervously.

"I think he's too injured for that," said Colter, his blue eyes twinkling. "Maybe he'll sense that we're trying to help him. At least I hope he will."

"If we leave him alone, he could die," said Tyler. "This is so rare; I'd like to try to help him if we can. We'll have to tell the ranger."

Huddling around the beautiful creature, the Warriors agreed to camp there that night and guard him from coyotes, bears, and other animals.

"Let's get him some water so if he wakes up, he'll have something to drink," said Tyler. Keeping constant pressure on the wound had finally slowed the blood soaking through the shirt. "He stopped bleeding, but he's already lost a lot of blood. Leave the gauze on, and I'll remove the shirt to wash it. He'll probably be weak for a while. Let's hope he wakes up."

"Jaguars used to be more numerous in southern Arizona, huh," said Makoa wistfully. "Too bad they're almost entirely gone now."

"Yeah," said Shawnee. "I guess they've all been trapped or hunted out for their skins, and to protect cattle. Or shot illegally, by people like that poacher Tyler helped Arizona Game and Fish arrest down south for killing a jaguar five years ago. How could anyone think of killing such a beautiful animal?"

They made camp not far from the jaguar on a higher, safer ledge covered by an overhang. Tyler set a pan of stream water beside the cat, and the Warriors used their filter to refill water bottles at the stream. Nobody got much sleep hearing the giant fanged beast breathing heavily nearby.

When the travelers awoke in the morning, the jaguar still lay unconscious.

"We're supposed to leave today," Colter said to Tyler at breakfast. "Our parents expect us back."

"I've been thinking about it," Tyler responded. "I've decided to stay here alone to help him recover. You three can hike to Shawnee's aunt and uncle's ranch and call Sierra for a ride back to Tucson. You'll make it easily by late afternoon, and if they're not home, go to their neighbors. All these ranch owners are good people, right, Shawnee? I've met them at the Easter barbecues. Tell them to call the ranger on duty. Tell 'em what we've got and where I am. Also, please ask Sierra to take care of Beau and to let the resorts know I won't be available the next few days."

"I guess we'll have to look for the Indian cave another time," said Colter.

"Probably so," Tyler said. "It'll keep."

The kids gave their leftover food to Tyler and finished packing.

Tyler instructed, "Remember to always stay together, within sight of each other, and no runaway leaders or left-behind stragglers. Got it? There should be some backpackers in the canyon if you need help, and you might even run into the ranger on patrol."

The Warriors nodded their heads, ready to head out.

As they said good-bye, Makoa warned, "Remember the forecast we saw before leaving; there might be a pretty good storm moving in. It's coming from the south and while warm, could probably get wet." After a pause, he added, "Don't get yourself eaten when he wakes up."

After the kids had disappeared from view, Tyler thought about Makoa's last remark, and a flash of doubt about his undertaking struck him. He quickly cast that feeling aside, knowing he could not walk away from the injured jaguar without deep, lasting regret. Surprised by his lack of fear and complete trust in his instincts, he took a long stick and pushed the pan of water closer to the beautiful beast. Somehow, he would nurse the jaguar back to health, and if necessary, he had his emergency locator device for rescue.

Tyler decided that he needed to have some food ready in front of the jaguar to start their relationship off on the right foot, so he gathered rocks for rabbit hunting. He didn't like killing anything, but the jaguar was too magnificent to let chance run its course. He hiked the short distance back to the main creek and then climbed up a steep side canyon that topped out above the cliffs. He aimed to reach flatter ground where there might be more game.

Before long, a rabbit bounded through the bushes and stopped under a small shrub some distance away. Tyler began stalking it, crouching low and staying out of view by keeping the bushes between himself and the creature. Noticing something red underfoot and hearing a loud hiss, he stepped back as a Gila monster retracted under a cholla skeleton. Its jaws opened wide, showing the black insides of its poisonous mouth. Tyler glanced up to see the rabbit running off down a gully and out of sight. He paused, marveling at the beautiful orange-red pattern on the slow-moving Gila monster's back; it looked like a painted Indian pot.

Hunting late into the afternoon, he finally succeeded in hitting a small cottontail, and like the traditional Indians, he said a silent prayer of thanks for the rabbit having given its life to help the jaguar.

Back at camp, everything seemed exactly how he had left it. The jaguar was still unconscious. He put the rabbit in a rock-lined cache beside the cool creek, finished his camp duties, and went to bed.

The Warriors reached Shawnee's aunt and uncle's adobe ranch house and rushed inside. The smell of mesquite drifted in the air as they hurriedly told their story around the long wooden kitchen table.

The last of the cracked red coals glowed in the beehive fireplace from the night before. Soon the phones were abuzz; the Warriors would stay there until Sierra came the next day in the early afternoon to pick them up.

Reaching the ranger on duty on this side of the canyon proved to be a harder problem. No one answered the phone at his house. In fact, no one had seen a car parked there for a week or two, and the distant headquarters in town were closed for the weekend.

The following morning, Monday, they got through on the phone only to find out that no one had been hired yet for the ranger position on this side of the canyon, and the ranger working the other side was out sick. As the Warriors waited for Sierra to arrive, they ate a rancher's breakfast and listened to the barrage of telephone calls. Meanwhile, the weather started to deteriorate.

Tyler awoke and started preparing breakfast. He took out his backpacking stove to boil water for oatmeal. On the way to the creek, he walked close to the jaguar to assess the animal's condition. Suddenly, the big cat's paw twitched! Tyler's hair began to rise. With a jerk of his giant head, the jaguar rose up on one shoulder, looked groggily around while sniffing the air, then rolled all the way up to a sitting position and found himself face to face with a human.

The creature's wide eyes seemed filled with both wonder and a sort of terror, and the sudden effort had caused noticeable pain. The jaguar looked down at his side where the sharp rock had punctured his hide. His dangerous eyes flashed up, accompanied by a warning growl.

Tyler quietly went to get the fresh rabbit and threw it gently toward the startled beast. Again the eyes flashed deadly danger, but when the cat saw the food, his glance changed to a puzzled look and slowly his demeanor softened. Failing to sense any threat, he leaned over but only sniffed the rabbit. Realizing his condition, he looked back at his wound and began licking it as if to change the subject.

Tyler sat watching, not daring to move. The giant predator rose to his feet with great difficulty and a low-pitched whine. A powerful exhale, like a deep echo from a cave, followed. Although an inner voice urged him to flee, Tyler sat still, his heart beating wildly. The jaguar took a short step, felt a sharp pain in his side, stopped to take a long look at Tyler, and then lay back down.

After continuing to look at each other for over half an hour, the big cat became even more relaxed. Then he reached over, snatched the rabbit in his mouth, crunched it up, swallowed, took a drink from the pan, laid his head down, and went to sleep.

The jaguar slept soundly, despite occasional loud exhales and twitching limbs. Tyler noticed the wind starting to pick up and high clouds blowing across the stretch of sky visible between the towering walls above him. With the storm coming from the south, there might be a lot of moisture, but the forecasters hadn't been sure where most of it would hit. They had said it could even fail to bring much rain to this area, but by midday the sky turned dark.

Weird, ominous highlights of smoky yellowish-green light swirled in the black clouds, belying some mysterious power as though the end was coming. The smell of rain came shortly thereafter. A few large drops started to fall, and then the sky unleashed a torrent of water. Long, glistening streaks connected the sky to the ground.

Tyler retreated to the shelter of his overhang, happy that his camp provided reasonable security. He kicked back and listened to the stark, lonely echo of a small waterfall at the back of the box canyon starting to trickle off the 50-foot cliff onto bedrock. Lightning flashed as hard rain fell. The jaguar, while under the overhang and mostly out of the rain, still lay in the path of some windblown spray.

After driving in a light drizzle through the verdant desert hills, Sierra arrived at the ranch beneath a steady downpour. She grabbed her straw hat and dashed inside. The strong, invigorating scent of creosote, activated by rain, hung in the air. Everyone rehashed the story while water boiled for tea. Sierra stared back out the window at the intensifying storm, surprised to see that the driveway she drove up just minutes before had turned into a lake.

They all debated Tyler's situation out there with the jaguar. No help would come from the rangers at this time, and rain continued to fall in steady sheets at an alarming rate. After hearing Shawnee's Uncle Ned warn that the clay roads would be slippery and probably washed out, it was soon obvious they would have to wait out the storm.

The kids called their parents to let them know they needed to spend the night once more, and everyone settled in to enjoy another evening of ranch hospitality. Shawnee's Aunt Pam already began serving homemade cinnamon buns and hot chocolate.

Heavy rain and thunder kept up throughout the night until finally around dawn when it slowed to a light, misty shower. Early in the morning, Tyler left Jag, for that is what he called him now, and went looking for rabbits again.

He traveled downstream to the main creek, which raged after the rain. He traversed on a raised terrace out of reach of the high-water, crossed it to the steep side canyon where water now flowed, and climbed nimbly to the top. He stood and watched while dense fog flooded the canyon from the opposite rim, temporarily filling the void with a thick white cloud, dissipating in spots and reappearing in others. Tearing himself away from this enchanting view, he headed off for the morning hunt in a fine mist.

Tyler came back with two cottontails at about noon. The jaguar jerked his head up and appeared a little startled and embarrassed at being caught napping, yet he remained lying down. Walking a few feet closer than previously, Tyler gently threw one of the rabbits to the huge cat. Jag started to stand, but the pain kept him down, and before long he ate the offering. Tyler cleaned the other rabbit and stored it in the cache. Still suspecting the jaguar might have suffered a cracked or broken rib and probably a concussion, he felt thankful that Jag was eating but also wondered how much longer the supply of rabbits would hold out.

That afternoon, the rain returned, falling as hard as ever. The already swollen creek began to roar, and the waterfall from the top of the box canyon now flowed about a foot across at the lip, crashing loudly on the bedrock below. The night passed uneasily for Tyler, who dreamed that the jaguar woke up and chased him. In reality, sleeping near the animal served the purpose of actually bonding them with trust.

On Tuesday morning, Sierra and the Warriors awoke and looked upstream toward the mouth of the canyon. Mist and low clouds hugged the surrounding mountaintops. Neighbors shared news of the nearby washes flooding across the road in two spots not far from the ranch.

After breakfast they decided to take a drive in the ranch truck to assess the situation. At the first big wash, the water had gone down, but more than a foot of sand and mud covered the road. Uncle Ned went back for his small tractor and worked to clear the way. He managed to open a passage in the first wash, but before he reached the second, the rain resumed with renewed vigor. They retreated to the ranch, leaving Ned's tractor in between the running washes.

By late afternoon, their dilemma deepened when they learned that the single bridge leading out to the highway had also washed out, along with a good portion of the road. Widespread flooding had stretched resources; help would not be available to Tyler until the road was cleared. Everyone settled in around the beehive fireplace with bowls of chili as Pam, Ned, and Sierra knitted their brows, trying to come up with a plan.

"You know," said Ned, looking at Sierra, "there's an old trail up to the rim from here. Once on top you can make it to that box canyon where Tyler and the cat are holed up."

"I guess someone should go see how he's doing," said Pam, "but not Sierra and the kids!"

"Sierra can take my rifle," offered Ned.

“I have some experience shooting,” added Sierra. “I grew up on a ranch.”

While putting a log on the fire, Ned lamented, "I wish I could go see that cat! Anyway, it'll be a while before the road is passable."

Leaning in, Shawnee spoke up excitedly. "We've been there already, and we'll be safe. Come on, Aunt Pam, we want to go back and check on Tyler. We can bring him more food."

"Sierra and the kids can get there safely by the ridge route," Ned said, trying to reassure his wife. "It's all high ground, and they can hike a small side canyon down to where Tyler is. I'll ride with them to the rim on ol' Apache; that mule knows the rough trails. But that's as far as I can go. My knees couldn't take that steep canyon down to Tyler. The trail sticks to the rim, and the draw down is marked by an obvious rock outcropping – a pointed pinnacle."

"Okay," Pam said, relenting. "I suppose that's the only thing to do. We're the only ranch this side of the wash-out. There won't be any help for days, and I don't think they'll spring for a helicopter in this situation."

"It's all right," Sierra reassured. "I know how to use a rifle, and we won't stay long. I just want to know that Tyler's okay."

"Me too," said Ned, shifting logs around with the fire iron. "The next two days are supposed to be clear before another surge of moisture. I'll pack some extra food for the jaguar if he's still there." After glancing at his wife, he added, "Sierra, just stay out there one night. There's a line of storms we're in the middle of. More hard rain might hit, but the satellite shows you have a good window tomorrow and most of the next day."

Pam gave Ned a defeated look and said, "I don't know what we're going to tell the parents."

"I'll help you call them this evening," Sierra offered. "I'll assure them we'll be safe." Unfortunately, before she could make the calls, the phone died due to complications from the storm. Their cell phones were also out of range.

The next morning, Pam waved from the porch as Ned, riding Apache, led Sierra and the three Warriors up the trail to the rim. The generous, experienced rancher had offered four packages of frozen venison for the jaguar. He rode with this bundle tied behind the saddle while the others carried backpacks with lightweight food and gear. At the top of the rim, they transferred the venison to their packs. With clear directions to the rock outcropping and down to the box canyon, Sierra and the Warriors stood ready to head off.

"If the jaguar already took off, eat that venison...and be careful," Ned instructed before making his way back to the ranch.

Jag awoke but did not raise his head. He just watched Tyler with his large, yellowish-brown eyes. Tyler spoke softly to his sharp-clawed companion as he guiltily prepared and ate his oatmeal. He then walked to the cache and retrieved the other cottontail. Jag was sitting up and waiting, a sign that he continued healing. Tyler took a chance, for he felt no fear in this moment, and walked right up to the jaguar while reaching his hand out with the rabbit.

A deep growl came from the cat's throat, and with noticeable effort he stood up. The two locked eyes for what seemed an eternity. Eventually, Jag warily took the rabbit from the offering hand with long, dagger-like teeth. Tyler stepped back, filled with the satisfaction that he had just made a great friend. The two rested throughout the morning, lulled by the sounds of floodwater roaring through the canyon.

In the afternoon, noises were heard coming from downstream. Sierra led the way, carrying the rifle while the Warriors followed. They approached quietly, not knowing what to expect, breathing hard and looking tired from hiking with heavy packs.

Tyler expressed surprise that they had been able to circumvent the flooded main canyon. Jag, still in obvious pain, rose and became alert at the commotion. However, when Tyler brought the group slowly and cautiously into camp, Jag merely stretched and looked on.

Sierra shared quick details about her last few days as they unpacked the venison and extra rations of freeze-dried food. Tyler immediately offered Jag a large serving of meat which he ate eagerly, straight from Tyler's hand. Looking on in amazement, Sierra and the Warriors also wanted to get closer to the beautiful creature but held back. Observing Tyler's interaction with the animal clearly demonstrated to them his brave, noble, and considerate nature.

"You're feeding him by hand. That's incredible," said Makoa.

"He trusts me now," Tyler said.

"I'd say the other way around, too" continued Makoa.

"Can you pet him?" asked Shawnee.

"I haven't tried that yet. I've killed three rabbits to feed him. He took one before from my hand, and now this."

"I'm glad we probably won't need the rifle," said Sierra. "Ned told me to bring it in case the jaguar didn't wake up in a friendly mood."

"How long can you stay?" Tyler asked.

"Just one night," Sierra replied. "We'll have to leave around noon tomorrow; another storm might be coming. Hopefully the road will be fixed by the time we're back."

"Wow, there's sure been a lot of rain," said Tyler. "Hope the parents aren't too worried, and boy, Pam and Ned sure are great."

Tyler started telling them about his last two days and Jag's progress, until he was interrupted by a funny whining sound. Looking over, they saw a playful, happy expression on the jaguar's face. The Warriors were not swayed to approach the large cat and took their gear up to the higher ledge where Tyler made camp. Although hard, flat bedrock spread over the ground, with sleeping pads they would make do.

Sierra and Tyler talked about what needed to be done.

"I'll leave you the rifle when I go back with the kids."

"I guess I better keep it, just in case," Tyler answered. "You know, the word jaguar comes from an Indian word meaning 'he who kills with one leap.' They have the strongest crushing power of all the cats!"

"Please keep the rifle handy." Her voice softened, "I've been worried about you, Tyler. I'm so glad you're all right." Tyler reached for her, and they held each other tightly.

Sierra wondered, "Hey, have you seen any sign of your cave, or whatever you think that so-called map leads to? Guess it's a great adventure anyway, whether you find it or not."

"You're right. A once-in-a-lifetime experience, rescuing a jaguar. No cave though."

Everyone gathered firewood and stacked it near the cooking area down closer to the injured cat. As they prepared dinner, the jaguar became alert, watching every move. Lit by firelight, the beautiful patterns on Jag's intent face stood out brilliantly. Sierra, Tyler, and the Warriors gazed back at him with affection. By the time the fire died out, the jaguar had fallen asleep, and everyone else selected sleeping spots on the ledge and tried to get comfortable. For a while, Tyler watched the almost full moon rise over the rim of the canyon. He then fell asleep and dreamed that the eagle map was meant to lead him to the jaguar.

The Warriors woke early and fed Jag by tossing the meat from the ledge above. As the sun rose to its zenith, the day warmed, and everyone lounged by a pool along the creek outside the box canyon. For an addition to their lunch, they enjoyed a hand-picked salad of miner's lettuce and watercress with a little mint thrown in. Before long afternoon arrived; Sierra and the Warriors had to go. They said their good-byes, already hoping to get back to see the jaguar again.

Noticing dark clouds moving over the canyon, Tyler spent the rest of the day gathering firewood and moving his camp down beneath a larger part of the overhang with a nice sandy floor. This natural shelter was at ground level, closer to the jaguar. Tyler trusted his instincts in reading Jag enough to feel safe at this proximity. Besides, he needed a more comfortable sleeping area. By sunset, the rain had returned.

Dawn finally arrived, and the jaguar slowly walked around in small circles. After carrying on all night, the rain still sprinkled as the temperature dropped. Water from the waterfall now cascaded down and around the big rock, collecting beneath the animal. Tyler stayed by his warm fire while Jag alternated between standing and lying on the wet rock, looking miserable. The clouds hung low; a menacing dark one, the size of a bus, rolled up the canyon between the towering cliffs above them.

In an instant, a loud "crack of the whip" shattered the silence. A lightning bolt shot out of the cloud and exploded with a puff of smoke on a nearby rock face. Three or four large rocks flew from the wall as Tyler fell backward in shock, and when he sat back up, Jag stood directly across the fire from him.

Instinctively, he reached for the rifle but realized that the jaguar had just been scared by the loud noise. Tyler felt no threat and decided to leave the gun resting on the ground. Eye to eye, the two of them sat out the rest of the storm under the overhang, dry and comfortable on the sand floor.

Tyler had collected a pile of clay from a nearby stream bank, and after lunch he began making pots to keep himself occupied. Time passed slowly as it sometimes does when alone in the wilderness. The jaguar, whose wound looked much better now, spent the rest of the day and night at the far end of the rock shelter, often shutting his eyes, resting, or sleeping.

Sierra and the Warriors reached the ranch, full of stories. Any progress made in clearing the road had been washed out by the successive storms. They were not getting back to Tucson anytime soon.

It rained again all night, but by morning the sky cleared, and Tyler looked up to blue skies and sunshine. The roar of the swollen creek in the main canyon filled the background, and that afternoon he decided to walk down and check it out, taking the rifle along just in case. To his surprise, the jaguar followed.

The turquoise lichen, and other greenery on the cliffs gleamed brightly after the rain. Tyler admired the lush scene while Jag walked slowly behind. As they came out of the side canyon, the experienced hiker was shocked to witness entire trees floating in the main creek. A waterfall created by the runoff of the previous night's rain cascaded off a distant cliff and ran to the canyon bottom. Large, bright patches of golden poppies, blue lupine, long-stemmed pink penstemons, and scarlet-red Indian paintbrushes highlighted the slopes. Tyler could not resist trying out some new spring grass, and when he lay down, he delighted in seeing Jag do the same about 20 yards away. They lounged in the grass for a good while. A little, bright flame-colored bird, the vermillion flycatcher, took off and darted around in front of them, catching flying insects before returning to his perch. Tyler noticed that the jaguar also watched the flying acrobat with intense interest.

They finally got up and walked a bit farther downstream. Jag suddenly stopped, turned, and started back. Tyler thought it best to follow since this marked the animal's first walk since sustaining his injuries and the sun had passed over the cliff wall hours ago.

Jag led Tyler around the edge of a giant rock and closer to the fast-moving flooded river. They made their way along a steep, slippery, and muddy bank. Tyler could see that this route would end against an impassable house-sized boulder and a deep eddy pool. He suspected the jaguar would investigate this fishing opportunity, then return.

Following to observe the cat, he set his rifle down on a bit of rock so he could use his hands in crossing the slippery clay bank. The jaguar dug its claws in, moving slowly and cautiously ahead. As they proceeded, each of them started noticing deep cracks widening in the bank and became alarmed. They only went a few steps farther when, in an instant, the entire section of bank broke away, sliding into the raging torrent – and taking them both with it. Tyler lunged for a log racing by in the current and held on for dear life. At the other end appeared the head and paws of the jaguar, with his hooked claws sunk into the wood and a wide-eyed look of child-like fear written plainly across his face.

Halfway submerged on the ends of the makeshift raft, they rode the rapids toward a cliff at the bend of the channel. Tyler pulled himself up on his elbows to look ahead and was shocked even more when he saw a roof of logs wedged between the canyon walls, forming a tunnel.

He could do nothing to stop the river from shooting them toward the menacing sight. The log jam must have occurred at the crest of the flood when the water measured 15 to 20 feet higher; it extended downstream for about forty yards.

They braced, preparing to shoot the tunnel when a strong eddy swirled the log toward an upright tree trunk leaning on the canyon wall at the bend, pinning them against it. The trunk forked 12 feet above them, apparently supporting the upstream end of this corner of the log jam. Stranded, both Tyler and Jag now crawled up on top of their log raft, which was now stationary, though quivering in the fierce current. For a moment they looked blankly at each other. Then Jag, who sat nearest to the washed-up tree, started up the vertical trunk by easily digging his huge claws into the weathered wood. As Tyler watched him ascend, he could see how the unstable, jumbled roof of logs created a possible death trap for him and the jaguar if the cat ventured onto it.

High overhead, stray clouds turned red in the sunset; night was coming. When Jag reached the top of the fork, he stepped cautiously onto the tangle of logs and debris that formed this dangerous obstacle. Startled into action, Tyler had already crawled along the floating log to the bottom of the tree trunk.

The jaguar began to shift his full weight onto the log jam, but Tyler jumped up and gave the cat's tail a quick warning yank. Jag jerked backward just as a giant log dislodged and plummeted down into the treacherous current. Many smaller branches followed, but miraculously the rest of the roof held.

The jaguar turned and settled into the upper fork of the tree trunk glaring at Tyler, who moved back to the far end of the log and tried not to stare back. Their eyes locked, though, and they seemingly looked deep into each other's soul. They telegraphed feelings back and forth, forming an intuitive bond that connected them on a deeper level. After several minutes, they lowered their eyes and rested, motionless. Blackness enveloped the bottom of the canyon.

They waited, trapped on the log. Soon the full moon appeared over the canyon wall and flooded the depths with light. Rough wavelets glistened in the moonlit river, weaving in among more subtly textured currents like the intertwining of silver among smoothly flowing ebony. It produced a stunning sight from their vantage point, so close to the turbulent surface of the river.

Tyler studied the current that had pinned their log to the tree trunk and rock wall. He tried to pull them upstream using small holds in the cliff, but he did not have enough leverage to break the eddy line and free the log. He and the great cat could only sit and observe patiently. The moonlight seemed to cast a spotlight on a small circle of water between the cliff and the log. It bubbled with life in an upswelling of current along the cliff wall. A frenzy of fish appeared in the sparkling moonshine, their silvery shapes and fins breaking the surface.

Jag zeroed in on the action with a one-track mind and began climbing down from the fork toward the bottom of the trunk. Just before moving onto the floating log raft, he glanced at Tyler, who instantly realized that he could harness momentum from the jaguar's jump to break the log free from the strong current. Turning away from Jag's stare, Tyler gripped the rock, looked over his shoulder at the cat, and pulled with all his might as Jag leapt down.

It worked! Now free, they were propelled into the main current and immediately met by a transecting rush of water. They kept death grips on the log as it bobbed up and down, flying through the tunnel. Shafts of moonlight shone surreally through the log roof.

Once the river swept them around the next bend and closer to shore, Tyler pushed away from the log and started swimming. Looking back, he saw Jag following. They coughed and sputtered onto a moon-lit beach and lay ten feet apart, utterly spent from the ordeal and now completely at ease with one another.

With the moon still high enough to see by, they made their way back upriver, Jag noticeably limping. Tyler retrieved the rifle. Back at camp they immediately surrendered to sleep. The two "shipwrecked" survivors slept almost until noon. When they awoke, both noticed a major change in the canyon; the roar of the floodwaters was gone. Tyler fed Jag the last of the meat, then "took" him for a short walk again. At the main canyon, the river's water level had dropped substantially. Apparently not fazed by water, Jag half-heartedly chased two large fish trapped in the shallows. It surprised Tyler to see him pounce lightly on one and eat it. The beast's exertions from the day before seemed not to set him back.

While watching the jaguar, Tyler found a few soft "pigment" rocks in the creek bed to make paint for his clay pots. This project could help keep him occupied while he waited for the big cat to fully heal.

That evening, he ground these softer rocks on the bedrock around him. Slight depressions, into which the dust collected, kept the various colors separated: red hematite-like rock, natural white chalk, yellowish rock, and charcoal. To add to his paints, he also gathered sparkling red "sand rubies" (actual garnets) from the streambed where they had collected in pockets within the sand. Using a metal camping plate and a swirling motion as if panning for gold, he successfully separated these small garnets and iron pieces from the lighter sand that washed out over the edge. Tyler then frayed the end of a yucca leaf for a paint brush. With everything ready, he added a bit of water to his powdered paints and began painting intricate native designs on the dried pots he had shaped the day before.

After resting for a couple of days, doing little besides eating good food and making homemade bread, Sierra and the Warriors still found the road impassable. With Uncle Ned's help, they once more set out on the trail back to the box canyon and their dear friend, again heavily loaded with supplies.

By afternoon they arrived, surprising Tyler who put this additional meat into the cool creek-side cache. He covered it using a heavy, flat stone for a lid. The Warriors stayed near camp with Tyler to rest while making and painting pots of their own.

The next day, they all decided to walk farther up the side canyon to the emerald pool and continue searching for caves. As Tyler packed daypacks, the Warriors painted stripes on their faces, looking wilder than ever. Jag watched their preparations and appeared ready to join them. Tyler brought along the rifle. Along the way, they explored a few empty caves and spotted others too high to reach. Their jaguar friend followed. The sun had just risen above the rim of the eastern cliffs, and when the Warriors reached the emerald pool, set like a blue-green gem between huge rocks, they couldn't wait to get in. They took turns jumping off the tall rocks while Jag lay watching from the shade of an oak tree. After swimming, the group spent some time basking in the hot sun, eating lunch, and stretching out for a nap.

Tyler dozed briefly but sensed it when Jag got up and wandered off; he kept a keen eye on him from his reclining position. The magnificent cat started up the side of the canyon and walked into a maze of boulders. Now and again, the creature appeared between openings in the rocks.

Jag moved across the slope leading toward the cliffs to where a spring dripped down the rock face, and when he disappeared into thick vegetation, Tyler roused the Warriors from their nap.

"Should we go see what he's doing?" he suggested.

"He probably knows a cool place to rest by that spring," said Sierra.

Not wanting to lose their friend so soon, the friends grabbed their packs and started toward the base of the cliff. Concealed by thick plants and the dark shadow from the overhanging rock, they followed a small game trail through the thicket and found themselves in a beautiful fern grotto. The fresh smell of the maidenhair ferns hanging from the wet rock mixed with the scent of columbines and monkey flowers. The large spotted cat was lying on a cool bed of moss, and when he saw his human friends approach, he gave that funny whine again. Deciding this meant the jaguar felt glad to have their company, the adventurers made themselves comfortable in the lush surroundings.

As Tyler settled the rifle on his knee, a tree frog started chirping from somewhere back in the ferns against the cliff. Makoa got up to find the little fellow, but before he could catch it, it jumped into a dark hole through a curtain of ferns.

"Tyler, hand me a flashlight, will you?" the boy requested.

Tyler fished the light out of his daypack and handed it to Makoa, who turned it on just in time to see the frog jumping down a small crawlway.

"This hole goes back!" he announced excitedly.

"Crawl in a bit and see if it turns into anything," Tyler said.

Holding the small flashlight out ahead, Makoa crawled in on his stomach while the others lounged with the jaguar in the verdant paradise of the grotto. After a few minutes, they started to get anxious. Tyler called Makoa's name, and upon getting no answer, he crawled over to the hole and looked in. He saw the light as Makoa came panting to the entrance.

"It's the cave, Tyler! This is the Indian cave! There are bows and everything!"

Tyler let out a whoop of joy.

"You showed it to us, Jag!" cried Makoa. "I can't believe it. You showed us!"

Jag looked at them with his head tilted and a funny expression on his face.

They grabbed their flashlights and, one by one, crawled in to join Makoa. The small entry tunnel squeezed tightly against them for the first ten feet, but then the cave opened up into a room. A little spring ran on one side; there were no formations, just blue-green undulating walls.

"Kokopelli!" exclaimed Tyler, pointing out the petroglyph. "This must be the cave we're looking for."

"Look at these bows!" prompted Makoa, standing on the far side of the room where seven painted bows leaned against the wall. The others joined him.

"They're beautiful," said Shawnee. "Look at the lizard symbol on this one. It's just like the design at the entrance to the mummy cave."

"These look like ceremonial bows," said Tyler, his eyes gleaming as he admired the finely crafted weapons.

Sierra knelt to study some chipped rock tools, but there did not appear to be anything else in the cave. The respectful adventurers left the bows exactly how they found them.

Colter, who had wandered off by himself, shouted, "A map! Here's another map!"

There on the rough, blue-green wall he had caught the light just right and found the faint depressions of another petroglyph. It also took on the shape of an eagle, crude in form because of the rough rock. A familiar arrowhead could barely be discerned on the wavy lines of the chest feathers. They examined the grooves in the petroglyph and wondered if another trail of adventure existed in their future. Tyler got out pencil and paper and made a careful sketch of the image while the Warriors continued to search the room. Finding nothing else, they crawled back outside.

"Well," said Tyler, "it looks like we might have another adventure ahead of us."

"Jag showed us this cave, huh," stated Makoa.

"It sure seems like it," Tyler replied.

The Warriors turned to the jaguar, and without thinking, Makoa reached out and stroked the big cat's head. A deep purring came from Jag as he rubbed his head on Makoa's leg. Sierra elbowed Tyler, who put his hand on the rifle. The rest of them stared in amazement; Makoa always had a special way with animals. Everyone wanted to pet the beast, but no one else had the nerve. Jag shook his head, then rested it again on a clump of moss.

Tyler, Sierra, and the Warriors were ready to head back. As they rose to leave their little "Eden," Jag rose to his feet and followed. At the emerald pool, they stopped for one more plunge, dried off on the hot rocks, and then started toward camp.

They spent the rest of the day swimming and resting on the sandy beaches close by. The humans occupied themselves making pottery and observing Jag, who seemed amazingly interested in all of their activities. Occasionally he would come up and rub against one of them, even allowing a tentative hand to scratch his back, signaling that total trust had developed. Twice he walked out of view for a short while, and the group let him have his peace.

The next morning arrived, like many other spring mornings in the southern Arizona canyons, with the wonderful sounds of birds calling in the surrounding trees. Still half asleep, Tyler identified the calls of the red tanagers and yellow warblers. Suddenly, he felt his face being licked by a large, rough tongue. Startled, he opened his eyes to see Jag's huge, beautifully decorated face. His heart smiled at such a warm greeting, but something made him wonder – was it a greeting or a farewell?

Jag walked from sleeping bag to sleeping bag, rubbing his big head against each of the sleeping Warriors and Sierra. Tyler put his hand on the rifle and watched cautiously. When the big cat came purring to Makoa's side, the boy awoke but remained still and echoed the same sounds back. The next few moments passed while the two carried on what seemed like a conversation. The music of their combined purring reminded Tyler of a tiny spring with a one-foot-high waterfall drilling into a small pool and echoing in a canyon wilderness. Their chorus of sounds stopped exactly together as Jag turned and bounded away, looking nearly as fit as the day they first saw him chasing bighorns.

The Warriors cooked and ate breakfast, stirred the fire, and talked about the jaguar's behavior and the mutual trust that developed. They loved him and hoped he would return.

Tyler and Sierra, overhearing their conversation, felt amused and touched by how much their younger companions cared about Jag. They felt the same way as the kids.

The day started to get hotter, and everyone wanted to hike to one of the pools for a swim. Around noon, they finally decided to go without their furry companion. It did not take them long to find him, however. Up the canyon and under a tree, they spotted the big cat lying on top of a juvenile javelina, proving he had healed and could once again care for himself. Watching him eat for a while and feeling a deep sense of pride that he regained strength from their efforts, they left him in peace and continued on to the emerald pool to swim. On their way back to camp, they saw neither the jaguar nor the javelina, which he had apparently carried off.

Jag, their friend of tooth and claw, failed to return that night, so Tyler decided he would go home with Sierra and the Warriors. As they hiked back to the van, Tyler could not stop thinking about the jaguar and the new map that would now challenge them. Like an eagle's talons seizing prey, daydreams of yet another adventurous quest took hold of him. He skipped down the trail, racing to meet whatever destiny lay ahead.

Photo by G. C. Grange

4

Rattler Cave

Life is strange with its twists and turns,
As every one of us sometimes learns,
And many a failure turns about,
When he might have won had he stuck it out;
Don't give up, though the pace seems slow--
You may succeed with another blow.

Success is failure turned inside out--
The silver tint of the clouds of doubt,
And you never can tell how close you are,
It may be near when it seems afar;
So stick to the fight when you're hardest hit--
It's when things seem worst
that you must not quit.
—from "Don't Quit," John Greenleaf Whittier

When Tyler got home, he eagerly took out the copy of the new petroglyph and tried to match it to his Arizona relief map, studying the rivers and canyons. Of course, many of the smaller creeks on the state map would not be shown on the petroglyph map. He followed the lines of the eagle's chest feathers and noticed progressively lighter and thinner lines branching off from the thicker segments. The larger grooves did match a major river on the relief map. Other markings pecked into the rock more or less corresponded with the faint lines of the river system's headwaters. The canyon marked with the familiar arrowhead lay to the northeast, and like the last one, it appeared to be a smaller side canyon off a main drainage. It showed up as a very short line on the petroglyph map and not on the relief map.

Once, long ago, Tyler had visited the larger canyon nearby, but he did not know of the smaller canyon marked with the arrowhead. He remembered that the country was rough and remote, cut with canyons, and filled with Indian ruins. The noise of a vehicle coming up the long driveway broke his concentration, and he went out to meet Sierra.

Sierra had come to bring Beau home. When he saw his master, the dog flew out the window and ran to greet him. Beau jumped all over as Tyler thanked Sierra again for all her help.

Later on, Tyler went to retell the story of the jaguar and report his finds in the Indian cave to his old dad, who now had his hands full of paperwork involving research grants and speculation from Tyler's data. It seemed so far-fetched that these eagle petroglyphs would turn out to be actual maps. Dr. Young could hardly believe this was the case, though he could only encourage Tyler to run with it after this second success.

For the next few weeks while the Warriors kept busy with school, Tyler guided resort guests and had barbecues with Sierra. In their spare time, Makoa took care of his pets, Shawnee rode her horse, and Colter played hard at soccer practice. They kept in touch by talking on the phone, interacting via social media, and occasionally attending each other's different sporting events.

Jag and the petroglyph never strayed far from their minds. Their eagerness to follow the new map motivated the group to plan their next adventure.

As Tyler drove Colter home from a game one week before their planned trip, Colter spoke hesitantly.

"I'm torn about going on this trip. We've got a big soccer tournament this weekend, and without me the team might lose, but I also don't want to miss an exciting adventure."

"Well," said Tyler, "I guess you'll have to weigh your feelings against what your mind says you should do."

Colter sat quietly, considering the alternatives, then he said, "You know what? There will always be another game; following the Indian map is a once in a lifetime opportunity. I may be letting the team down a bit, but if I'm not there, someone else will get a chance to play. It's not all about winning."

"Making decisions in life is often tough," Tyler said, "but as you gain confidence and faith in your reasoning and see that things often work themselves out, you'll become an accomplished decision maker."

The week rolled by quickly. On Saturday morning Tyler and the Warriors loaded their supplies in the van and left early. After driving a few hours, they turned onto a steep dirt road.

The track climbed out of the desert, through the oak and shrub forest, and up to the thick pine-covered slopes. There was still evidence of the desert biome here, with prickly pear cactus and agave growing among the trees.

The road paralleled a clear stream lined with giant white sycamore trees, then ascended a rocky rim, and eventually came to the edge of a huge waterfall. After stopping, looking around, stretching their legs, and admiring the falls, they hiked up beneath a bright red cliff to a small ruin and looked out over the distant, intermingling ridges.

The sun prepared to drop below the horizon, and the old rock walls of the ancient ruin in front of them glowed with the last golden rays. As the sky turned a deep crimson, they ran back to the van and headed up the mountain to flatter country. Passing through beautiful meadows flanked by tall pines, Tyler pulled off at a good spot to camp. They were high atop the Mogollon Rim, a steep escarpment that stretches halfway across central Arizona. It felt much cooler at this elevation, so they needed a fire for staying warm and preparing dinner. The next day they would explore the steep, rugged canyons that dropped off this rocky rim in search of whatever the petroglyph might lead to.

Darkness crept in around them, but as the fire grew, it lit up the surrounding meadow and forest. After dinner the Warriors, full of youthful energy, took out the instruments they had brought along and played hard for over an hour. Colter and Shawnee took the rhythm and worked a steady beat on their guitars as Makoa produced an ingeniously agile fiddle lead.

After sorting camp gear, Tyler joined in with his harmonica. At one point, feeling the energy of the music, Makoa jumped up on a big log near the fire. With bent knees, he sawed his fiddle with incredible speed. This sent the others into a powerful rhythm, taking all their strength.

Colter's beat-stomping foot started to dig a hole in the ground. When Tyler jumped into the lead to trade licks with Makoa, the harmonic effect put them into a musical trance. Their sounds traveled out into the still forest, a special music to be heard only by the nature spirits.

The song stopped as if it had a mind of its own, and the musicians gathered around the fire and shared deep sighs of contentment. One by one they went off to their sleeping bags until only Tyler remained by the fire. Staring into its smoldering embers, engrossed in the intricacies of color and texture, he paused to appreciate how deeply he loved life at that moment.

After a quick breakfast, the Warriors readied their daypacks and Tyler affirmed their plan to be back by nightfall. The adventurers anticipated a long day; they would be dropping into a deep, steep-sided canyon and might be hiking back late, so they all packed headlamps with fresh batteries and extra flashlights just in case. Plus, there might be caves.

Tyler also carried his usual equipment for exploring: a few candles, a first aid kit, and fluorescent-topped popsicle sticks for marking trails at night or in caves. Because of the very steep country and possible cliffs, they carried two ropes, one of standard thickness measuring 100 meters, and the other a thinner 50-footer.

They prepared their lunch and water bottles for the day, then the Warriors cleaned up around camp, picking up even the smallest pieces of paper, plastic, and tinfoil.

Tyler led them to the beginning of a faint game trail that would eventually descend between massive cliffs to the bottom of the steep canyon. Beau raced through the meadows beside them, leaping with the joy of being free in the wild, until a strange call from the treetops stopped everyone in their tracks.

"Listen," whispered Tyler. "I don't recognize that call. Let's see if we can find who's making it." Moving quietly toward a tall pine, they looked up to where the sound came from.

"There! In the top of the tree! See the shiny dark green and red? It's a trogon! I can't believe it. Tyler continued, "This is one of the rarest and most exotic birds in Arizona. They winter in Mexico, and some summer in our higher, cooler mountains of southeastern Arizona. This one is slightly north of its normal mountain refuges."

Leaving the beautiful trogon in peace, they returned to the game trail and followed it through the woods along a ridge between two canyons lined with sheer cliffs. Undaunted by the thick plants starting to obscure the trail, they managed to bushwhack down to a rocky ledge.

Tyler decided to explore along this ledge, since it cut back into one of the canyons and provided an opportunity to travel fairly easily on mostly flat rock. After working carefully around a couple of bends, he spotted a stone tool.

"Look! A scraper! A sign of Indians."

"And here's a piece of corrugated pottery!" Shawnee exclaimed, holding the artifact for closer examination. She suddenly shrieked and threw it down. "That scorpion almost got me!"

"Yeah, they often cling upside down under rocks and wood," Tyler said. "Watch out!"

"Maybe this ledge was a trail used by the Indians," Colter wondered aloud.

"Probably," Tyler uttered.

They continued traversing along the ledge, encouraged by their finds. More stone tools and bits of pottery appeared while the adventurers picked their way across rockslides or worked around cacti blocking the path.

Upon rounding the next corner, a glance upward revealed the somewhat intact multi-story stone walls of a cliff dwelling. The mud and rock ruins were tucked high into a wide crack in the cliff, and the approach led the group up difficult scree from the fallen walls and collapsed beams of several roofs.

They decided to climb around on the bedrock to the stabilized top room which was wedged under a large overhang. At this elevated spot, Tyler and the Warriors crouched on their heels imagining the native people who, like them, gazed out over the canyon, though hundreds of years earlier. The thought of these people living in this isolated sanctuary left them awestruck and silent.

They looked down through two large rock formations directly in front of the ruin to the deep canyon gorge that dropped steeply away. Resembling two sculpted eagles, the rocks framed the view of lush greenery and tall vine-covered trees filling the canyon bottom.

"What a spot! It's like an eagle perch. And look! Those are the eagles!" said Shawnee, pointing toward the rock formations.

"Eagle Ruins," Makoa announced, suggesting a name.

Tyler, looking out past the eagle rocks, spotted something. "Look! Across the canyon, between the eagles' feet...see that dark hole in the rock face? Looks like a cave."

"You think so?" asked Colter.

"Well, you never know," Tyler replied. "It could be just a shadowed crevice. Let's remember that large reddish outcropping above it so we can check it out when we get over there."

The Warriors searched around the Eagle Ruins for a while, finding large metates, scattered pieces of pottery, stone chips, small corn cobs, and yucca fibers. They examined the well-constructed roofs made of large smoke-stained timbers and smaller interlocking split yucca and agave stalks, topped with a mixture of clay and dirt.

When they convened after their survey, Tyler instructed, "The ancient people who once lived in this cliff dwelling and others along the Salt River have been termed the Salado, meaning "the Salt People."

Thinking out loud, Makoa said, "Can you imagine living in this rugged rim country all your life, hiking these steep trails between pine forests in the high country and the canyons far below? Wow! What a physically demanding life. They must have been tough people."

Tyler and the Warriors backtracked along the ledge to the steep ravine and then climbed or slid their way farther down using trees and shrubs as holds. Almost to the bottom of the canyon was a small game trail that traversed the slope through a jungle of vegetation. Wild grape vines hung from huge trees beside the trail, and the happy gurgle of a stream, still 20 yards down, echoed off the canyon walls.

Taking the trail upstream, Tyler spotted large tracks pressed into the mud. "Looks like the black bears are about the only visitors this canyon gets." They all bent down to examine the large tracks and measured them in amazement with outstretched hands. Tyler knew that the rugged canyon had seen few recent visitors by the looks of the trail, and the bear tracks provided further proof.

Hearing splashing water, they continued up the canyon to a spectacular waterfall cascading off a high cliff. The trail, no doubt an old Indian route, led directly behind the falls under an overhang. This path continued back down the canyon on the other side, while the bordering stream angled sharply down.

"Let's have a look at the eagle map," Tyler said. After splashing their faces in the waterfall, they sat in the shade of a huge oak beside the cascade.

Enchanted by this remote and hidden canyon paradise, the Warriors stared through the falling water down the canyon as Tyler took out the tracing of the petroglyph.

"The map shows a side canyon branching off from this one, but I don't remember seeing any. The topo map doesn't show a side canyon either." Tyler felt a little disheartened but determined to search anyway. "Come on, you guys," he said. "Let's keep going. We can see more ruins up ahead."

Beau led them along the small game path. By the time Tyler spotted the large black snake in the middle of the trail, it was too late to call his dog back. He held his breath as Beau ran right over it! The snake hurried across the trail and slid under a rock as Tyler approached. He identified it as an Arizona Black-tailed Rattlesnake and felt relieved that Beau had not touched it. Unless being handled, a rattlesnake will generally only bite after being stepped on. For this reason, Tyler nearly always led the way while hiking with the Warriors in rattlesnake country.

Most of the time, as in this case, a snake will either lie perfectly still until danger passes or sound the alarm with its famous rattle. However, sometimes the creature will just give a warning click or two, a signal which an experienced hiker can distinguish, even from the rattle of a dried seed pod.

Tyler had walked by many rattlesnakes over the years, and whenever he heard the click of those rattles, he went airborne and bounded away. Tyler and the Warriors never killed rattlers, respecting their right to live, but the explorers sure kept a sharper eye out after being reminded of their presence.

Hiking on, they kept looking for a break in the canyon wall. As the path penetrated the deep brush closer to the cliff, they saw another group of Indian ruins tucked up under the overhanging wall. The rock and mud houses remained in good shape with their doorways, beams, and roofs still intact. Although Tyler had not ventured here for years, he remembered that the old village stretched for 50 yards or so along the base of the cliff. The Warriors scattered as they set off to explore the mysterious beauty of the wondrous, ancient earthen homes overgrown with trees and vines. The cliff dwellings were positioned on the north side of the canyon in accordance with native custom. During the winter, the sun sits lower in the southern sky and shines into the homes, warming them up. In summer, the sun is higher, and the overhang casts a shadow on the living area, keeping it cool.

On this spring day, the sun shone against the front walls and partly into the rooms. As they walked through the ruins, the group saw the usual manos and metates, pot shards, stone tools, and scraps of woven yucca. The rock wall forming the back of the living space displayed several red handprints among other pictographs.

Many springs flowed along the rock overhang housing these ruins. The water nurtured yellow columbine flowers, maidenhair ferns, mosses, and other greenery around a small, crystal-clear catch pool. This clean, earth-filtered water was safe for drinking, and the adventurers stopped to fill their bottles. Meanwhile, Colter walked over to examine the rock wall of a nearby ruin and spotted some handprints in the clay plaster.

Tyler guessed, "Those are probably from 500 to 1450 A.D. Their hands, you can see, made little prints; people in general were smaller than we are now."

"Here are even smaller ones," observed Makoa. "They must have been left by children."

Shawnee walked back to the front of the ruin and scanned her eyes across the rugged canyon landscape. "Look!" she yelled. "I think I recognize some granaries. This village ran down both sides of the canyon. Maybe they stored food on the other side."

The Warriors gathered around Shawnee to observe the distant structures. The creek had cut down from their level and now ran a hundred yards below them. Staring across and taking in the whole scene of this paradise enclosed by towering cliffs, they fell silent.

The canyon's "music" filled their ears with nature's tranquil sounds: the gurgling of the creek, the crashing water from the far-off falls, the leaves rustling in the breeze, the buzz of insects, the singing and chattering of birds, and the cry of freedom from a distant hawk. Tyler came up and stood quietly with the Warriors. Listening to the remote sounds of the canyon filled them all with inner peace. For each one of them, to experience a place so completely felt like an awesome, sacred gift. The stream of sound from nature's countless instruments flowed into their minds, hearts, and souls, bringing them in tune with the canyon and one another. For these wilderness explorers, the talent for keeping silent held as much importance as speaking mindfully. With the magic moment ending, Tyler decided he would add to the background music and took out an Indian flute from his pack. Sharp notes sailed out over the chasm like the scream of an eagle. Stopping suddenly, Tyler's last notes were left floating in the canyon's echoes before fading into the scenery, lost forever in the wilderness.

Rising from their meditation, they again set off on the path along the canyon wall and after rounding a slight bend, found yet another group of ruins. Tyler looked up to admire the smooth cliff above the old houses: an artistic masterpiece with mineral stains painted steadily, over eons, by water running down the rock.

"Hey, look at that crack in the cliff behind the ruins! I've never noticed that before on other trips. Let's check it out!" Tyler suggested.

They discovered that the crack, mostly hidden by brush, measured about ten feet wide and ran at a steep angle up into the cliff. They climbed the first 25 yards or so with little difficulty.

The narrow slot continued, but Makoa looked up and announced, "There's the red overhanging rock we saw from the Eagle Ruins!"

"And maybe a cave!" said Tyler. "Let's see if we can climb up there. Perhaps this is the side canyon we're looking for. Let me put the harness on Beau."

Tyler tied a safety rope to Beau's harness, and they all climbed up to the reddish rock, crawled across a narrow ledge beneath the overhang, and came upon the large dark hole seen from the Eagle Ruins.

The shrill, descending song of a canyon wren echoed among the cliffs as they peered into the dark hole. A steady warm breeze flowed out of the deep darkness, indicating a long passage. The Warriors quivered with excitement.

"Let's go in!" Tyler declared, already digging into his pack. "Everyone, check your headlamp. We'll leave Beau tied up here, out of danger from mountain lions. Test all of your extra flashlights, too."

Soon everything was ready to go. They looked out from the cliff over the beautiful canyon paradise and listened to the distant waterfall one last time before entering the dark underworld. Everything seemed so bright and safe on the outside compared to the dark, cool rocky hole they prepared to enter. From the cliffs above came the sharp cry of warning from a hawk or eagle. Gathered together, the adventurers clicked on their headlamps and began creeping into the rocky passage. One at a time, they crawled to the first small room and grouped up.

"There are no petroglyphs or sign of the Indians so far," said Tyler. "Living so close by, they must have known of this cave."

"I hope it's the one we're searching for," Shawnee said. "If not, it's still cool."

The Warriors worked their way through three small rooms, crawling between them by way of tiny tunnels. The first few caverns were rather dry and lacked formations, but the next room they entered was full of white stalactites hanging from the roof and stalagmites rising from the floor. The sparkling white walls gave the larger room a dream-like appearance and excited them at the prospects of this "wet" cave. Everyone now realized from the enticingly beautiful live formations, still forming drip by drip, that some exciting discoveries could lie ahead.

Tyler knew caves and used good judgment when exploring them, including avoiding death traps with unstable rocks. He stayed away from mine shafts which often house old, rotten timbers supporting the roof as well as deadly gases that can kill quickly. However, some deep natural passages in the earth become "cemented" solidly together by leached limestone that over centuries flowed and dripped like candle wax, creating fantastic and beautiful shapes. These caves are safer to explore, and Tyler took his chances for their scenic rewards.

People often refer to wet caves as "crystal" caves because everything sparkles and shines. The formations inside often appear pure white or sometimes crystal clear in color.

These caves form in limestone from which water leaches the calcium carbonate to produce the formations. When these formations dry, not only do they stop growing and lose their color, but they also become worthless for collecting. This reason alone should deter people from breaking and taking these natural wonders, and in many places, laws also exist to protect caves and the formations within them. Of course, some caves do contain large quartz or other types of crystal deposits that formed through different processes.

Passing through this "White Room," they came to a steep climb, and Tyler led the way up the wet, slippery 30-foot wall. After anchoring himself at the top with a smaller rope tied around a stalagmite, he belayed the others up.

"I'll break out the trail markers from here on. This cave is already getting tricky," he said, placing one of the popsicle sticks capped with fluorescent tape at the top of the climb to mark the way back.

They chose a route that looked particularly inviting with a possible chance of going deeper. The passage went on for some distance, winding through rooms of various sizes. Wherever interconnecting tunnels offered alternative routes, Tyler left a marker. The trail of reflectors leading back out of a cave always provided reassurance by functioning as a collection of true beacons of safety.

The explorers passed through a room containing large, wavy sheet-like curtain formations that hung down from above. In addition, a 40-foot, pure white stalagmite stood alone in the center of the cave floor.

"Wow!" Colter said, walking up to the sparkling rock. "It looks like a giant goddess."

"Be careful not to touch the formations; mud can stain them for years," warned Tyler, who like the rest of them was covered with mud from crawling.

They continued for another hundred yards or so, either on all fours or walking, when possible, until they came upon a rock wall with a very small hole at the bottom.

After stopping to examine the opening, Tyler said, "I'm afraid we've reached the end of the easy going in this direction. I wonder if this tunnel connects..." He bent down and looked in. "It looks like it might extend a ways."

The Warriors felt nothing but skepticism for the very tight passage until Tyler led the way without hesitation. They hung back in case he could not clear the narrow opening. Sharp rock cut into his elbows and knees, and he broke into a sweat. It was definitely a tight fit, but Tyler forced himself through the entrance and kept on crawling, hopefully along a route to something interesting.

At one point the passage seemed to be too narrow, but he found a depression that his body could fit into with his head turned sideways and slowly worked through it. Trying not to think about the coffin of rock encasing him, Tyler blocked out negative thoughts as well as one could. He wiggled on, feeling as if his body and mind were caught in a tightening vise. He wondered whether he would be able to move backward through such tricky spots. While working past the squeeze, he paused often to make mental pictures of his position, study his immediate surroundings, and calculate his retreat.

Satisfied with the possibility of retreat, Tyler pressed on around a slight bend and felt utterly shocked to see, through the end of the small tube, only blackness. He moved on toward the odd-seeming dark void. Upon climbing through the hole, his light faintly hit the farthest walls, revealing a huge room.

Facing back into the lengthy tunnel, he yelled, "Hey, come on! A giant room!"

As Tyler waited for his young friends, he stared in amazement at the countless columns, pillars, and chandeliers that comprised a mysterious landscape of unbelievable beauty. The multicolored rock glowed white, yellow, orange, and red as his light played among the formations.

Massive rock "curtains" and "organs" hung from the walls, and the ceiling looked like an enchanting upside-down stalactite forest. One by one the Warriors crawled through the tight hole and sat on a ledge in awe of the wonders before them. Eager to explore, they started down the wall using a "ladder" of stalagmites for holds. The room's flowstone floor looked so smooth that it appeared to have a candy coating.

"Let's take our muddy boots off," Tyler said. "We shouldn't get this beautiful floor dirty."

After tying their boots onto their packs, they continued exploring barefoot. Tyler and the Warriors wandered between giant snowy-white stalagmites that towered above them on all sides. They traversed up and over slopes of candy-like stone, taking in the scenic wonders all around them. Delicate miniature fantasy worlds existed in the smaller nooks and pockets, some full of crystal-clear helictites: formations that grew from the walls like tentacles, weaving in every direction.

Makoa asked, "How is it possible for helictites to grow in different directions, like a plant?"

Tyler explained, "Minerals dissolved in water are apparently squeezed out like toothpaste from the unsolidified center tube in each formation. They dry at various angles, resulting in these fantastic shapes."

The explorers took great care not to touch the incredible works of art, built with time and seen only in the depths of Mother Earth's underground galleries.

Makoa came across some smooth, round cave pearls scattered in small basins.

"What are those?" asked Colter.

“Well,” said Tyler, "they look like real pearls from oysters, but cave pearls are formed when loose bits of foreign matter, such as sand, develop successive coats of calcite from the mineral rich water which gently splashes down from the roof. The splashes also tumble the growing pearls and polish them.”

Beyond the next little rise in the floor, the group discovered a clear pool with a delicate crystal rim. An adjacent flat, dry area provided a good place to rest. Tyler took out several candles which everyone helped to place around the room in prime locations.

"Put some aluminum foil under each candle so we can catch the wax," instructed Tyler. "Anything foreign, even the wax from candles, will grow a fungus in this moist environment. I've seen a peanut left on a cave floor covered with a halo of five-inch-long hair. Another time, I saw a dead bat turned bright green by a strange growth. Leftover wax turns black, leaving an ugly scar on formations.”

“Gross,” said Colter.

Once all the candles were lit, the Warriors took off their headlamps, used the bright beams to illuminate the most interesting parts of the room, and settled down for a snack.

“This is the most beautiful place I've ever seen,” sighed Shawnee. "I'll try to describe this to my parents, but I know I couldn't even come close."

"Yup, it’s hard to explain all that you really see and feel on a fantastic adventure,” Tyler responded. “Mother Nature reserves her greatest gifts for those who look the hardest, the lucky souls willing to put in the effort. And like a wise old gypsy, she shows you just a little at a time, which naturally keeps you coming back."

The Warriors sighed, having heard this saying before, and continued munching on nuts, chocolate, and dried fruit while gazing in wonder at the incredible cave formations. Tyler took out his harmonica and played a quiet song, breaking the profound silence of the cave. This day perhaps marked the first time since the cavity’s formation that the lights and sounds of people occupied its depths. There were no signs that Indians or anyone had come to these deeper inner rooms; not a single track showed in the mud.

Beneath hundreds of feet of rock and dirt, the group now experienced one of the greatest sanctuaries on earth, so far from everyday life. Here, as in any wilderness, humans could feel on their own, free of society's bonds.

A sense of freedom enveloped the Warriors, and this sentiment manifested itself in Tyler's hypnotic music. The sound waves were absorbed softly and entirely in the perfect acoustics of inner earth.

As Tyler really got into it, Colter, Shawnee, and Makoa lay back and observed the fantastic candlelit room with its crystal-clear pools and surreal backdrop. They felt transported to a distant land, and in this exotic environment, the pure sound of the music reached unusual heights.

With great versatility, Tyler breathed his emotions through the harmonica. Everyone fell into a state of bliss until the music wore out. Tyler lay down with the others to rest and enjoy the view. Once complete silence took over the Warriors' private paradise, their feelings indeed seemed too deep for words.

Suddenly, strange sounds began coming out of the large organ-shaped formation hanging from the roof. The cave was playing its own music! The spellbound adventurers directed their gaze upward as a series of beautiful fluid notes ran up and down the scales, resonating from the rock. Then a narrow stream of water came pouring out from the lowest point of the organ and into their midst.

By some strange coincidence, water released from above had streaked through capillaries within the rock, reverberating it with sound. The delicate "trilling" sound, which only nature could have achieved, lasted maybe ten seconds but would be remembered forever by those who heard it.

The explorers shared a wondrous, fleeting feeling – a secret knowledge that the earth was, in fact, alive! After a deep sigh of

"Ahhhhh" and a moment of reverent acknowledgment for the miraculous occurrence, they settled back against the rock.

"Imagine what amazing, inaccessible underground worlds there must be," said Makoa.

"How would you like to travel in an earth-boring machine with instruments to detect open pockets deep underground...discovering giant crystals and beautifully decorated rooms of different colors?" Colter dreamed.

"That sounds cool," said Shawnee. "You could have lasers and high-tech boring teeth."

"One can only guess how many miles of passages there are, decorated with fantastic formations. I'd like to be on the crew of that first earth-sub," Tyler mused. Then after a pause, he suggested, "Let's go look around a bit more."

They gathered the headlamps and spare flashlights and left their other gear among the burning candles. At the entrance to a small, narrow tunnel, they stopped to admire a tall wall covered with twisting and turning large white helictites.

"This is a masterpiece," said Shawnee. "Look! Antelope antlers!"

"And there's a unicorn!" said Colter.

"Unbelievable," uttered Makoa.

"Let's see where this tunnel goes," suggested Tyler. He began carefully sliding and climbing down a steep slope with the Warriors right behind him. When the passage led him into a tiny room, he excitedly aimed his flashlight at the roof.

"Wow!" Tyler exclaimed. "Check out these orange crystal-spiked clubs. I've never seen this type of formation before!"

Colter's stomach growled as he said, "This floor looks like peanut brittle; it's honestly making me hungry."

They came out of the room and decided to explore another passageway that spiraled upward like a staircase. Tyler left a trail marker where the passage forked and led his friends through delicate milky-white formations called "soda straws" that extended from roof to floor.

The route ended in a small room with shallow depressions, each filled with fragments of crystallized rock. At one time these little pits had been pools of water with crystals growing along the edges and floating in "rafts." The explorers settled into this comfortable room with its low ceiling of stalactites and looked through the calcite crystals. Makoa, however, noticed a dull glow coming through a small opening and went to have a look.

"We're above the big room," he said. "I can see light from our candles." The others came over to join him on the hanging balcony that overlooked the immense illuminated formations.

Makoa added, "It looks like the grand room of a palace, and we're in the jeweled balcony."

At that very moment, several bats flew through the picturesque scene. As they soared and glided enchantingly across the big, candlelit room, Tyler recalled some knowledge about the creatures.

"The Maya Indians deified bats and often carved them into their stone artwork. They thought of them as mystical animals, representing supernatural powers and death. If we had their powers of memory for acoustic landmarks, we wouldn't need trail markers to remember our way."

"Yeah, I guess echolocation alone wouldn't cut it; in this maze with all the side passages, they'd be lost forever," put in Makoa as the Warriors watched the scene with wide eyes.

Shawnee added, concluding the theme, "The death part probably came from the bats' night habits, living in what ancient people thought of as dark scary holes. I think bats are awesome and of course useful pollinators and insect eaters."

Then the adventurers retraced their steps, confidently following the trail of fluorescent taped sticks down the spiral staircase to their candle camp. Many cavers have been tricked by subtle forking of passages, especially when covering great distances and as fatigue sets in, but Tyler's markers kept them on course.

In the big room, they rested for a while before packing everything, including their candles and wax, and then prepared to explore further.

"We haven't seen any sign of the Indians yet," said Tyler. "I wonder if they could have made it back this far. I doubt it. I've heard of Natives going deep into caves using bundles of dried cane-type plants for torches, but it's hard to imagine superstitious, primitive people taking the risk to get this far."

"If the Indians left anything in this cave, it could take a long time to find," said Colter.

"That's for sure, in this maze! Shall we check out that passage?" Tyler indicated with a nod as he started for a far corner of the room with a large, obvious tunnel, but they discovered that this route soon ended. While poking around, Colter discovered a hidden passage behind a giant slab of rock. They all ducked into it and found themselves crawling along on hands and knees through soft, comfortable clay.

A series of uniquely decorated large rooms and halls gave them the opportunity to occasionally walk. Tyler pointed out some of the geologic wonders along the way.

"Look, a crystallized aragonite "bush" growing from the wall... And here, this roof is pure red ochre..."

"Man, that's rich colored clay," Makoa commented.

Tyler led on and continued, "Guys, have a look at these bands of hydromagnesite, this shaving cream-like substance called "moon milk" with bulbs of crystallized rock growing from it."

Confronted with a few small crawl spaces, Tyler again marked their chosen trail with a fluorescent stick. The tunnel began to angle upward, forcing them to climb in many places through sharp rock until the route leveled off and again turned to a clay floor. However, the sticky, sucking clay was so thick that everyone sank several inches and could hardly move his or her feet.

Shawnee suddenly called out, “Hold on! I lost a boot.” After a few moments of pulling it out of the clay, she confirmed, “Here it is. I see rock up ahead; I’ll put my boot on over there.”

"What's that?" Tyler blurted out in an excited but hushed voice. Seemingly out of place, a strange dull light glowed up ahead.

"Turn your lights off, everybody!” he instructed. Beyond a bend in the passage, the eerie light was incomprehensible; their hearts froze. The unexplained glow, truly mysterious in its quality, jarred Tyler's memory.

"It's got to be light from the outside!” he announced. “We must be near an opening!"

Tyler cautiously started forward with the Warriors trailing directly behind. As they entered another small room, the light gradually brightened. They immediately noticed stone tools and large pieces of pottery scattered on the floor and dropped to their knees to examine them.

Deciding to see where the light emanated from, Makoa proceeded through a narrow vertical squeeze and entered a room where daylight flooded in.

"Come on! You've got to see this!” he yelled as he walked across the room to a window-like opening in the rock that looked out over a slot canyon. From the higher vantage point, Makoa recognized the scene below as an extension of the same slot canyon from where they had entered the cave.

He turned around and spotted a painted pot sitting on a stone shelf across from the window. As he moved closer to examine it, a sound like the ripping of a bed sheet behind him caught his attention.

He spun around in time to see the tail and wingtip of a golden eagle swooping by. Startled by the unexpected meeting with a human, the great bird flared its wings and let out an ear-piercing scream while it struggled to fly up and out of the narrow cleft.

Hearing the eagle's war cry echoing sharply through the canyon and ricocheting off the cliffs, Tyler, Shawnee, and Colter hurried into the lit room. Makoa was already leaning over to analyze the pot on the ledge. When he told the others how he had just barely seen the eagle, they quickly glanced out the window opening and then set off to find discoveries of their own. Right away, Tyler spotted the familiar petroglyph on the wall. With a broad grin spread over his face, he stood before the "map," noting the faded arrowhead on the eagle's breast.

He scanned the room until his eyes fixated on the familiar red Kokopelli pictograph, then went to work tracing the petroglyph. Shawnee and Colter knelt beside another large painted pot found in a far corner.

For a few tranquil minutes, everyone focused intently on the cave treasures that represented such a deep connection with the past. Abruptly, a familiar and dreaded noise rang out. The Warriors looked up and saw Makoa face to face with another large Black-Tailed Rattlesnake. Apparently, the reptile had been coiled on the ledge behind the pot, as if to protect it.

The cornered snake lashed out at him, and with the agility of a small monkey, Makoa instantly leapt toward the far wall. The others rushed over as the fleeing snake slid off the shelf and headed straight toward the boy, now trapped in the corner.

Without allowing himself a moment to think, lest his hands betray him, Tyler moved with lightning speed and grabbed the rattler by the tail just before it reached Makoa. The dangerous reptile's head reared back at him, but with a quick jerk, he flung the loudly rattling snake out the window. The rest of the group stared, astounded, as Makoa rushed to Tyler's side. Then, everyone broke into excited talk.

"I was just starting to pick up the pot when I saw the snake curled up next to it!" exclaimed Makoa. "Thanks for saving me!"

"I didn't know if he was going after you or not," said Tyler. "I just decided I had to do something."

After they had calmed down a bit, Tyler's attention turned toward the intricately designed pot on the stone shelf. Reaching out and touching the rim of the ancient work of art, he started saying, "What awesome craftsmanship this is..."

When, "Thiiiit!"

Two large, curved fangs darted from the vessel and immediately sank deeply into the back of his hand.

"Ayeee!" Tyler jerked away, but the entire writhing snake remained attached and hanging from his hand. While Tyler continued to retreat, it extended two or more feet before releasing its grip and coiling back into the pot.

Tyler yelled in anguish while hideous rattling echoed from within the vessel. He grabbed the pot, shook the snake out over the cliff, and then collapsed to the cave floor.

His stricken hand began to throb intensely. Tyler knew that rattlers sometimes inflict only a dry bite without using their venom, but as the pain increased, he lost this hope. He also recalled that when one encounters a rattlesnake, its mate may lurk close by, but he never expected to encounter one inside the pot.

Realizing that he urgently needed to receive treatment from a doctor, Tyler suggested rappelling down and added, “Then two of you can go for help. I can’t believe it...two Black Tails.”

The Warriors estimated the drop from the rock window to the cliff’s base to measure short of fifty feet, so their doubled 100-foot rope would suffice in length. Makoa secured it around a large, sturdy stalagmite and remembered to tie the ends together before throwing down that part of the line. This prevented anyone from accidently rappelling off the end of the rope.

Once the last adventurer successfully lowered, they could untie Makoa’s knot and pull on one end to retrieve the rope. As Makoa threw the knotted ends over the edge, he looked down and noticed two broken-off poles lashed in place with yucca fibers.

"Look, you guys. These must be the remains of an old Indian ladder." His friends came over to see before busying themselves with their own preparations.

Then one by one, the Warriors threaded the rope through their figure 8 belay devices and carefully rappelled down the cliff face. Colter used the thinner safety rope to belay Tyler's rappel while his injured friend struggled to simply hang on.

Tyler's pain spread rapidly as the venom traveled up his arm. Colter rappelled down last and finished pulling in and coiling the rope as the others slowly made their way back to the main canyon.

Tyler spoke up, "I shouldn't go much farther. Hiking out will radically increase circulation and spread the poison even more."

The steep climb out of the canyon posed too much of a risk; he would have to use his GPS rescue locator and wait at the ruins for rescue.

Colter climbed up to the cave mouth to untie Beau, then went to refill everyone's canteen from the spring. Makoa and Shawnee helped Tyler to lie down beside some ruins under an overhang and near a dripping spring.

He turned to the Warriors and suggested, "You'd better gather a lot of wood; we're going to need a fire burning all night." By the time the sun set, they had a large pile ready. Tyler made sure he had a clear view of the sky for a satellite to mark their location, and then he pushed the red button for rescue.

As blackness of night filled the canyon depths, the rock wall of the overhang lit up as if by a spotlight. An owl's hooting call echoed into the distance.

With Beau at his side, Tyler stayed awake late into the night, hoping the locator would bring a timely rescue and coping with the intense pain the best he could. The Warriors kept a close eye on their friend. In the firelight, Tyler's tensed muscles, veins, and leathered face looked more rugged than ever as he endured the effects of the poison.

Finally, the Warriors fell asleep curled up by the fire while Tyler stared, half-hypnotized, at the glowing bed of coals. He tried to keep his weary mind off the pain by searching the embers for shapes and faces.

A jaguar's head emerged, rippling in stunning shades of red and yellow as the fire's heat pulsated. Around the jaguar a jungle of trees, vines, and other plants appeared.

For the time being, Tyler lost himself in his visions and imagination, and his pain faded into the background. Next, a raised temple materialized behind the jungle scene; the coals had cracked and stacked perfectly to form a flat-topped pyramid. Other details in the richly colored scene gradually came into view, and a feeling of bliss blanketed him. Then the temple collapsed, revealing in its center a bright yellow, glowing cave that looked like a route to the molten fires deep in the earth. The jaguar's head glowed brighter.

Tyler could not shake the feeling that these "visions" were more than a mere hallucination from the venom. Even in his dire situation, he tried to stay positive and hoped the venom might actually help him to "see" in some way. Closing his eyes, he settled into the earth while old memories filled his mind with vivid images of Mayan temples.

Abruptly, Tyler shouted out, "Jaguar Temple!"

Still half asleep, Colter bolted upright at Tyler's announcement and asked, "Are you okay?"

No response came from Tyler.

"More firewood?" Colter asked instead.

"Sure," said Tyler, wincing as the pain returned in full force. In less than a minute, the newly fueled flames warmed them up and illuminated the cactus-hung cliffs.

Now witnessing Tyler's intense pain, Colter repeated sympathetically, "How do you feel?"

"Pretty bad," Tyler groaned. "My whole arm is throbbing. I hope we get help soon. Feels like the longest night of my life, enduring every second."

"Hang in there, Tyler! Help is surely on the way."

"Colter, I want you to take the new petroglyph map and keep it safe while I'm in the hospital. Hide it at your house until I get home."

The boy nodded in reply and did as his mentor requested. Soon Colter fell back asleep, but not Tyler, whose low moans could be heard throughout the canyon as the night wore on.

Helicopter
Pete Connolly

5

Rescued -- Ambushed

Destruction and greed
will often rule man.
Unless for the sake of good
he takes a stand.
Working for harmony
with nature, and the land.

Tyler, Beau, and the Warriors spent the long night close to the fire, and their spirits lifted when at last the birds began chirping and the sun rose. They got up to heat some spring water in their metal drinking cups. Tyler had noticed some sage growing nearby, and the Warriors made tea with the leaves to warm them up. An earthy aroma drifted through the air as they sipped the hot, soothing drink. Tyler's badly swollen arm hung limp by his side, and the sweet-smelling tea allowed the pain to ease out of his mind for a moment.

A distant sound, hard to identify, came drifting into the canyon. Then from high over the cliff wall, a loud, startling, and repetitively rhythmic noise shattered the peace of the canyon; thankfully, here came the rescue helicopter. The pilot easily followed the smoke rising from the campsite far below the high cliffs and under the overhang.

He lowered the helicopter into the canyon, moving slowly along the rock walls. From the air, the world below looked like a garden of Eden hidden within a fortress of towering cliffs and spires. The creek, emerging from the upper canyon in a sparkling waterfall, turned into a silver snake as it ran down in the sunlight.

Awed by the beauty and remoteness of the hidden paradise, the pilot uttered a single, almost inaudible "Wow." He slowly brought his craft to a steady hover near the overhang, where Colter stood waving his arms. Tyler remained by the fire.

The doctor on board, however, looked at the canyon scene with less appreciative eyes. Failing to take in the beauty of the place, he wanted to be done with this inconvenient rescue mission and get back to his more profitable practice in Tucson. The doctor had begrudgingly accepted this position as part of a plea bargain requiring many hours of community service. This allowed him to keep his medical license despite his arrest for hunting and killing an endangered species.

After scanning the terrain for a safe landing spot, the pilot settled on a huge flat rock located downslope from the overhang. He cautiously sized up the situation, then approached carefully. He worked the controls with an expert and delicate touch to successfully land the chopper, and the rescuers disembarked.

Tyler painfully watched all the action while the Warriors worked to put the fire out, not an easy task given the large pile of coals that built up over the long, cold night. Using drinking bottles to carry water from the spring, they repeatedly doused the coals and stirred them into the dirt until the fire was completely out, knowing that if they left even one live coal behind, a strong wind could blow the ember into dry brush and start a devastating wildfire.

The doctor and pilot soon joined them. Introducing himself as Dr. Shaw, the thin, wiry man with a scraggly beard bent down to examine Tyler. Something about his quick eye movements caused Tyler to instinctively feel distaste. Shaw's eyes darted from place to place, never resting for long on any face or allowing anyone to see into them, to read his soul.

Before arriving at the scene, the doctor glimpsed Tyler's name on some paperwork and entered a mild state of shock at the coincidence. Tyler Young was the same name that appeared on the ranger's report when Shaw got caught shooting a jaguar.

The two had never met face to face, and the newspaper printed neither one of their pictures at the time of the incident.

"When were you bitten?" Dr. Shaw asked, again averting his gaze to avoid meeting Tyler's piercing eyes.

"Yesterday afternoon."

"Where were you when it happened?"

"Down by the stream," said Tyler, not wanting to reveal the cave's location.

"Could you tell what kind of snake it was?" Shaw asked.

"I'm sure it was an Arizona Black Rattlesnake."

While Dr. Shaw examined the badly swollen hand and arm, Tyler clenched his teeth at the slightest touch. The doctor decided that the antivenin shot could wait until they got to the hospital in case Tyler suffered an allergic reaction to the medicine. However, Shaw stressed that they should waste no time in transporting his patient.

With one of them on either side, the pilot and doctor loaded Tyler into the helicopter. Shawnee, Colter, and Makoa buckled in with Beau across their laps. While they rose above the canyon, the doctor asked Tyler what brought them to such rugged country.

“Just a backpacking trip,” Tyler moaned, feeling the pain shoot through his limbs as he tried to talk over the noise.

The doctor pressed on. "I saw those ruins. Did you find anything interesting?"

"Always! But nothing really. Just the cool ruins," he answered impatiently.

The pilot radioed the ranger couple on watch at the fire lookout on the summit, and they agreed to look after the kids and dog. A parent and Sierra were tackling the three-hour drive to pick up the Warriors and Tyler's car.

After dropping off Beau and the Warriors at the fire lookout, the helicopter flew Tyler directly to Tucson, leaving him alone to deal with his pain and worries. The hospital staff administered the antivenin shot and held Tyler for observation. Exhausted from staying up all night, he finally fell asleep despite the intense pain. The nurses who made rounds that evening found him thrashing about wildly and muttering in his sleep; they called Dr. Shaw, who was still on duty.

"Where's the cave? The Indian cave! We found it!" Tyler said over and over. Dr. Shaw stood by the bed and leaned forward, his nose like the beak of a roadrunner ready to strike, as he wondered what Tyler was talking about.

"The eagle petroglyph! Follow the lines; it's a map. They're rivers... Mummies... Look, Sierra, giant painted pots filled with crystal arrowheads! Turquoise beads!"

Dr. Shaw excitedly pulled up a chair and took a seat.

"Snakes!" Tyler yelled. "Watch out for the snakes!"

Deep in his dream, Tyler saw the shaft of golden light come through the roof of the mummy cave and shine on a large arrowhead.

"A giant golden arrowhead! We can't take it. Don't tell anyone."

Shaw's sole interest in life was money, and though he felt hooked on the idea of finding priceless gold artifacts, nothing about prehistoric Indian cultures interested him one bit. He sat stone still, his mind now filling with images of a lost Indian cave and golden treasures. Tyler and the Warriors must have found something special in the canyon, he thought.

As Tyler continued rambling about a lost cave, rattlesnakes, and Indian artifacts, Dr. Shaw began seriously thinking about this cave in which, quite possibly, Tyler's snake bite had occurred. Maybe an entrance lay near the same overhang where the helicopter rescue took place. Lured by the prospect of riches, Shaw made up his mind to find out more.

Once Tyler stopped talking in his sleep, Dr. Shaw left the room. Tyler went on dreaming, now of his friend Jag traveling along a beautiful riparian stream and swimming in pool after pool with river otters scattering before him. The jaguar climbed out of the stream and then went high above a great canyon onto a shelf of limestone covered with fossilized shells.

Tyler woke up thinking about Jag and longing to see his feline friend. If anyone could have kept track of the jaguar's movements, they might conclude that the great cat also possessed highly developed senses and feelings for his human friends.

Some mysterious forces apparently drove Jag to deviate from his normal range in southern Arizona and travel north. After reaching the Verde River in central Arizona, he continued upstream, often swimming and encountering otters as in Tyler's dream. Likely killing deer and javelina along the way, he veered northwest through the canyons, mountains, and plains toward the Colorado River and the Grand Canyon, the northern extent of jaguar territory in the fairly recent past.

The next morning, Dr. Shaw came in early. Tyler noticed quite a change in his personality. He seemed overly friendly and talkative, eagerly asking questions about their camping trip. Although a little suspicious of this change in character, Tyler felt a lot better and did not mind talking. Of course, had Tyler realized this doctor's identity and moral history, he would have been much more wary.

"How much of the canyon did you explore?" Dr. Shaw asked.

"Oh, just the way in and a little bit around the area where you found us."

"That's a beautiful canyon," the doctor continued. "I bet you could find Indian relics in a place like that."

Hoping to evade further questions, Tyler said, "We did find a couple pieces of pottery and some chipped stone but not much else, except of course the beautiful canyon and waterfall."

Dr. Shaw turned his attention to Tyler's hand and said he was relieved to see how much the swelling had gone down.

"You're lucky," Shaw reminded him. "There probably won't be much tissue damage since you received a fairly small dose of venom and the antivenin took effect immediately." The doctor continued to ask more prying questions such as how far Tyler's group hiked and in what direction. Shaw's odd air and sudden interest in the canyon gradually raised Tyler's suspicions; something seemed amiss.

Sierra and the Warriors stopped by to visit just as the doctor was leaving. On his way out, Shaw greeted them and made small talk about their activities. A couple of minutes after he left, a static sound came from an unmarked box mounted on the wall next to some other equipment. Tyler gave the device a quick glance before dismissing it from his mind, and before long the friends began discussing their discovery.

"The map is hidden at my house," said Colter.

"Good. Keep it safe," said Tyler. "I've got to get back as soon as possible to pick up the trail markers we left. If hikers stumble onto that cave, they could follow our trail to the hanging window and the petroglyph map."

"Can we plan on returning the weekend before Memorial Day?" suggested Makoa. "I'm going with my family to Sedona for the holiday; we're staying at a cabin by the creek. Maybe Sierra can go into the canyon with us this time and stand guard alongside Beau?"

"I'm certainly willing," offered Sierra, "but let's make sure Tyler is well first."

"By then I will be," Tyler said. "We can leave early that Saturday and be back by late evening. It'll be a long day, but it's the only one I have off from guiding."

"That's the one upcoming weekend I am free, too," Sierra added.

"I'd love rappelling out of the window again," said Shawnee.

Colter, always excited by a challenge, blurted out an energetic "I'm in!"

Shawnee continued, "But you know what? This time I want to hang out with you, Sierra, on the lookout."

"Do you want to go, Sierra?" Tyler asked.

"Sure, no problem. It'll give me time to kick back in the meadow and work on my book. Shawnee and I will have a happy time hanging out with Beau. Tyler, we've got to get going now; it's time for me to take these guys home."

The box on the wall crackled once more, an unexpected clue that their conversation had failed to be kept private. After Tyler's wild thrashing and sleep talking episodes, Dr. Shaw had ordered a sound monitor turned on at night. When the Warriors gathered in Tyler's room, Shaw asked the nurse to retrieve some records from down the hall. Meanwhile, he promised to watch the desk while finishing his paperwork – and slyly switched on the monitor in Tyler's room.

The following day, Dr. Shaw released Tyler from the hospital but could not release the new information from his mind. He became consumed with the idea of following Tyler and his friends back to the canyon and thereby discovering the location of the Indian cave. He relished the thought of exacting a measure of revenge on Tyler.

A few days after returning home, Tyler invited the Warriors over for a map session. Colter brought the tracing from their newly named Rattler Cave that Tyler passed along to him for safekeeping, and they all gathered around it. Tyler laid his trusty Arizona relief map beside the hand-drawn reference, and everyone fell immediately into deep concentration.

Again, the lines marking the feathers on the eagle's chest corresponded almost perfectly with major river systems, but this time they overlapped with the northwestern part of the state. This new "map" clearly showed the Grand Canyon, with the arrowhead indicating one of its largest side canyons. Tyler carefully marked the spot as accurately as possible on the topo map and then sat back in his chair.

"Well, Warriors, we've got another cave to search for."

Colter exclaimed, "I don't believe it!"

"Incredible!" put in Makoa.

"Another cave!" said Shawnee, brimming with emotion. "I can hardly imagine another quest filled with adventure, like the last."

"Or as physically challenging," Colter included.

"Well," said Tyler, "anything great or rare is usually difficult to come by."

"So, when can we go to the Grand Canyon?" Makoa asked Tyler.

"That will have to wait until the end of June when I'm done guiding. The trip will probably take a week or more with searching and all. But in the meantime, we really need to go back to Rattler Cave and pick up our trail markers."

Satisfied with their rough game plan, the four friends parted ways for the night.

Tyler scheduled a meeting with his worried mother and father. They talked at length, and Tyler filled Dr. Young in on the latest cave discovery and the new petroglyph. The archeologist took detailed notes on the information from Tyler's survey and added it to his lengthy report, tying things together.

Tyler returned to the hospital during the next couple of weeks for follow-up visits. Dr. Shaw overheard him telling a nurse that he would be out of town hiking and would miss out on a blues concert that she mentioned attending the Saturday before Memorial Day weekend. The doctor felt pretty convinced that Tyler still planned on returning to the Indian cave in the canyon, like he had overheard while eavesdropping. As the time drew nearer, Shaw contemplated the best way to follow Tyler and his friends. Trailing them in the canyon without being seen could prove nearly impossible, but if he set out a day early, he could get there ahead of time, find a place to hide, and hopefully watch their every move.

Harvey Shaw gathered his supplies, including a rope and some climbing gear from college days. He also packed binoculars for scanning the hillsides, a skill he had learned while hunting.

The doctor planned to stay hidden in an elevated spot with a good view of the canyon and little chance of being spotted. He could simply sit back and watch while Tyler and the others made their way to the cave. He would rent a car to help cover his tracks and hide his identity.

On Friday afternoon, the day before Tyler's expected approach to the cave, Dr. Shaw parked his rental car behind a clump of trees bordering the apple orchard and set off with his pack on the canyon trail. An hour or so later, he reached the rim and looked into the depths until he recognized the spot where the helicopter had landed. Shaw hiked cautiously around the head of the short, steep canyon and out along the far rim. He nervously glanced back from time to time, fearful that Tyler might have decided to come early. Eventually, he stopped at an overlook with a good view of the chasm yawning beneath him and decided to take up his position there.

Dr. Shaw ensured that no sign of his camp remained visible from across the canyon where his quarry would approach. Satisfied with his cover, he settled down behind a rock and scanned the opposite slope with his binoculars. He took out a book to read but kept vigilant watch throughout the afternoon, looking up now and again to scout. As night fell, he cooked his dinner and wondered what the next day would bring.

Tyler, Sierra, Beau, and the Warriors left for the remote canyon at dawn on Saturday morning. Parked at the trailhead, Sierra and Shawnee settled to wait. After a quick safety meeting, Tyler and the two boys headed into the canyon, moving rapidly down the steep ravine.

High above and hidden in the rocks, Dr. Shaw eventually picked up their movement. A flicker of sunlight reflected off his binoculars as Tyler and his friends descended into the lush growth. They passed in and out of sight between bushes and rocks, but Dr. Shaw had little trouble following. Before long, the group reached the canyon floor and the waterfall; Shaw briefly lost sight of them, but they soon appeared on the slope almost directly below. Scared of being sighted, the doctor found an old tree near the edge of his perch and peered through its branches. He lost the "Apaches" again when they passed through the ruins and made their way up the steep side crack to the cave. He ran nervously to different parts of the cliff and cautiously peeked over the edge, but Tyler's group did not re-emerge. Shaw heard nothing but the occasional rattling of rocks falling below.

Growing tired of waiting, the doctor went back to his camp, grabbed some food from his pack, and returned to the steep side crevice where the rocks had fallen. He kept a sharp eye out, wondering if the cave might be down there.

He spotted sudden movement, and to his surprise, he saw Tyler standing partway up the cliff face, apparently in a cave opening.

With the excitement of a hunter sighting his lost prey, Dr. Shaw became careless in his concealment. Luckily for him, Tyler seemed occupied uncoiling a rope and did not look up. Realizing his careless exposure, Shaw quickly moved behind some large boulders and stopped to take in this momentous realization. The presence of a secret Indian cave rendered him nearly breathless. Waves of excitement coursed through his body as he envisioned the treasures that awaited inside for the taking – unless Tyler had swiped them already. The doctor even recalled Tyler talking about a petroglyph map and another cave to be found.

While these thoughts raced through his mind, Dr. Shaw watched Tyler toss the rope down the cliff, clip in, and rappel from the cave. Makoa and Colter quickly followed.

Shaw stood up to look farther into the crevice where they carefully descended. Surprisingly, the large boulder he had chosen to hide behind and lean his weight on suddenly shifted!

Like a dark cloud covering the sun, an evil idea came into his mind. His position aligned directly above the spot where Tyler and the Warriors rappelled from the opening, and with a slight push, the boulder could tumble down on them. If he could hit Tyler, all competition for the golden artifacts believed to rest in this cave, and in any subsequent hideouts that the petroglyph map might lead to, would be eliminated. He completely ignored the possibility of hurting the kids. Moreover, Dr. Shaw felt tempted to finally get back at Tyler and exact revenge for their past encounter when his life had nearly been ruined.

Dr. Shaw caught a glimpse of Tyler reaching the ground and starting to pull the rope in. They would soon be on their way. Sinister thoughts rushed through the mind of the doctor. His greed and desire for revenge became too great for his twisted brain to resist in this wildly opportunistic moment. Placing his hands firmly on the large boulder, he rolled it off the ledge with a shove. The giant rock crashed against the cliffs with a nightmarish sound, bouncing about as if of its own volition, before smashing into a thousand pieces on the bedrock. A loud echo resounded throughout the canyon.

Dr. Shaw lay flat, not daring to look down to see if he had hit his human targets. If they remained alive and saw him on the cliff's edge, he would be in for some real trouble. Hopefully the seemingly naïve bunch would view the incident as a natural rockfall in this steep, isolated canyon. Crawling back to his camp like a snake among the rocks, the doctor continued to lie low and pulled his gear in tightly around him, maintaining cover from every direction. He would risk a look down into the crevice later. Right now, his conscience expressed real anguish over his actions; he was wracked with worry.

Dr. Shaw waited, paralyzed, for over half an hour before daring to glance over the boulders concealing him. He watched for movement on the slope where Tyler and the Warriors had originally descended into the canyon. They should be climbing out by now if they somehow escaped unharmed. He continued to watch the trail for another silent, worry-filled hour.

By that time, Shaw felt convinced of hitting his target, and he nearly yelped aloud when his eyes processed a flash of movement. Fumbling for his binoculars and smashing them against his face, he gasped at the sight of a strong mature mountain lion climbing the steep incline. He sighed with relief, lamenting his decision to venture into the canyon without a firearm.

Not a single thought of appreciation for such a rare encounter with nature crossed his mind. A minute or two later, the lion disappeared over the hill, but something else appeared at almost the same instant. Disappointment replaced the guilt of his evil deed as Dr. Shaw identified Tyler and his two friends, none of them injured, moving up the slope. An unavenged feeling of revenge and greed returned to eat at him, though the doctor figured this ordeal ended quite fairly; at least now he knew the location of the cave.

Dr. Shaw decided to spend another night in the wilderness. He could not risk running into his intended victims, and the next day he planned to rappel down to the cave and see what he might find.

Dawn broke with dark red filling the eastern sky as the doctor lay dreaming about the possible treasures hidden in the cave. He bore no curiosity about the ancient ones who had placed their beautiful pieces of art in the caves. Instead, his thoughts fixated solely on money. When Shaw peered out from his hiding spot, the sky appeared fire-red, fully ablaze, but he did not even pause to take in the beautiful scene. He just quickly lay down, cursing the cold.

Dr. Shaw had never really developed a close connection to nature, and it showed in his inability to appreciate beauty in the natural world. He only tended to venture out of doors to shoot or hunt, not to enjoy the land or the wildlife. Nor did he particularly care for the raw, athletic challenge of stalking an animal while hunting, a deeply instilled element in the lifestyle of men for most of their time on earth. Shaw only went out to violently plunder and needlessly lay to waste another animal's life due to some sickness of the spirit. He often killed game out of season, left dead animals on the ground, and simply shot at whatever moved if boredom set in. He held absolutely no respect for earth's creatures. Perhaps past experiences of a type deficient in anything positive or loving had shaped his bleak, narrow outlook.

As soon as the sun peeked over the horizon, Dr. Shaw packed his gear and set off to look for a safe spot to rappel down. He walked around the head of the small slot canyon where he had spotted Tyler in the natural window. The doctor found a sturdy juniper tree to pass his rope around and positioned himself directly above the opening in the rock. He threw the tied ends down, and the rope just reached the cave window. After shouldering his pack and hooking up his rappel gear, he lowered himself over the cliff.

Reaching the cave, Shaw untied and immediately saw the painted pot on the ledge. He wasted no time wrapping it in an extra shirt, then stuffing it in his backpack. Continuing to search impatiently but figuring that Tyler and his group must have taken everything else, Dr. Shaw missed the other pot. In fact, Colter and Shawnee had concealed the precious artifact behind a slab of rock. However, the doctor did notice the eagle petroglyph and remembered the map of river systems described by Tyler in his fitful sleep. The arrowhead displayed on the eagle's chest appeared exactly how Tyler had unwittingly reported.

After making a detailed copy of the petroglyph, Shaw caught sight of the passageway leading deeper into the mountain. He traveled down it a little ways until stalactites started appearing on the roof. Seeing no more Indian treasures, he broke off a couple stalactites and put them in his pack. Of course, he did not consider that by doing so he robbed the cave of beauty that took untold years to create. Furthermore, the doctor was unaware that the broken formations would quickly dry out, losing their luster and appeal. He retraced his steps for fear of getting lost.

Back at the window, Dr. Shaw pulled his rope down from above, wrapped it around a stalagmite, and rappelled out of the cave. As he hiked back to his car, he felt a sense of accomplishment. He found no golden artifacts, at least not on this mission, but he did leave with a priceless pot and the map to another Indian cave.

After topping out and getting back to the meadow, Tyler and the two boys told their story to Sierra and Shawnee.

"We rappelled out of the cave," explained Tyler, "then all of a sudden, I heard this crash above us. Without thinking, I dove into a small crack about three feet high, maybe six feet long. To my surprise, Makoa and Colter beat me there."

"There was another crash right beside us, like a bomb exploding," said Colter. "The whole ground shook! We must have bounced up a couple inches."

"Sounds of shattering rock echoed through the canyon like a machine gun," Tyler continued. "Fragments of the canyon walls flew everywhere; some small pieces even hit us. Odds are it was just a natural rockfall, but while hiking out, we glimpsed a mountain lion on the slope above us."

"Perhaps he was stalking you and accidentally dislodged some rocks," Shawnee said, voicing everyone's conclusion.

"Maybe...or ambushing us," joked Makoa. "Whatever happened, we were lucky."

"It's amazing that you reacted so quickly and luckily had a hole to jump into," Sierra added. "Sounds like you could have been chopped to pieces by flying shards of rock."

"Well," said Colter, "we retrieved the trail markers from the cave. At least our secret will stay safe."

Or so they thought.

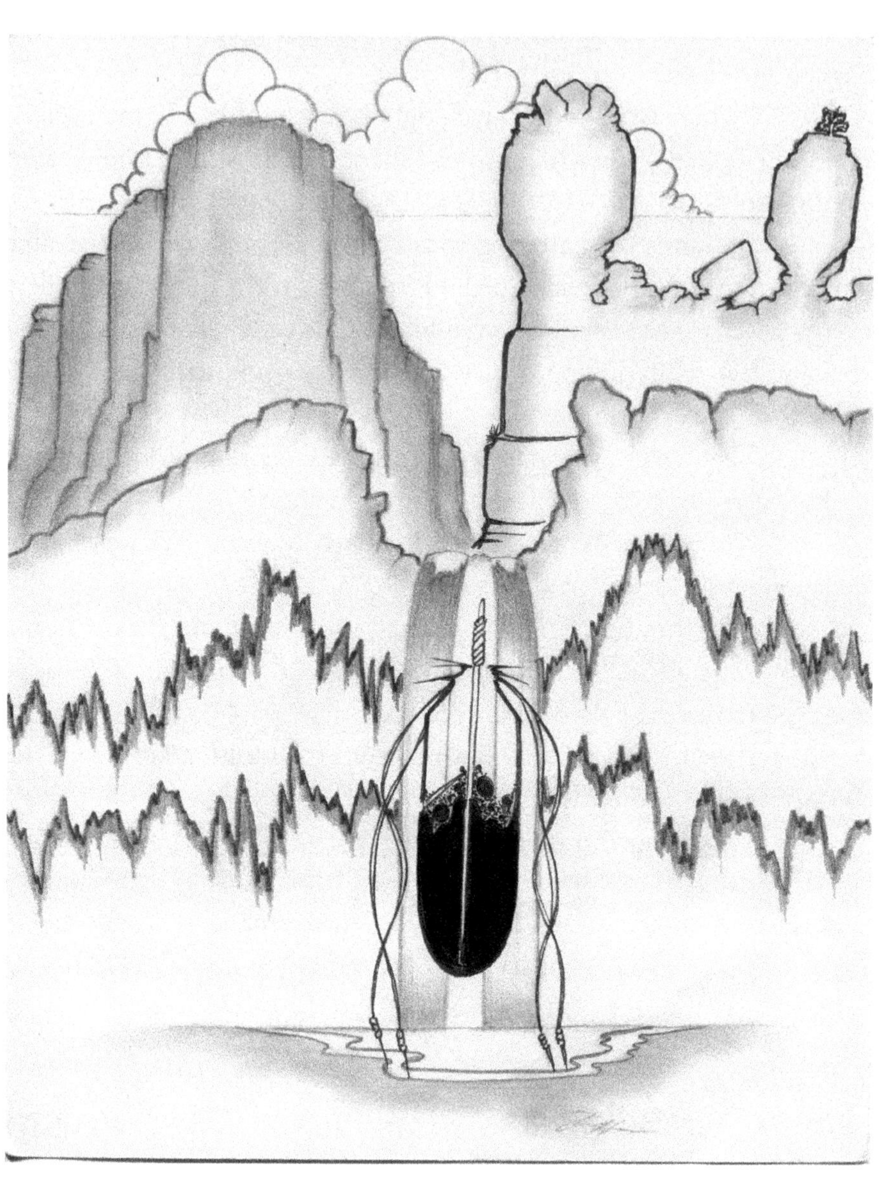

Eagle Feather in Falls
Jasper Hanna, Havasupai

6

Turquoise Waters

Drawn to places akin to their own wild spirits,
the Warriors' souls were branded
with magnificent images of the wilderness.
Nature stirred their imaginations and emotions,
each adventure restoring inner peace,
stimulating new goals.
They became attuned to themselves
and the Earth.

School was out for the summer, so Tyler and the Warriors took their time deciphering the new map. The arrowhead definitely marked the Grand Canyon's largest side canyon, the home of the Havasupai or "people of the blue-green water." This stunning, mystical canyon paradise resembles a real-life Shangri-La.

The Native American tribe, which traditionally referred to itself as Havsuw 'Baaja (the Blue Creek People), initiated a tourist enterprise for travelers who want to camp and hike in beautiful Havasu Canyon. Thankfully, they also recently recovered some of their ancestral homeland on the upper rims of the canyon.

The Warriors had four long weeks to wait before their trip to the Grand Canyon, one of the largest canyons in the world. The Havasupai termed it "the great-grandmother canyon" after living atop and within its depths for generations. Because it provided such profound isolation, these people remained one of the last Indian tribes to be influenced by European cultures.

While making plans and gradually preparing for the trip, Tyler worked on throwing one more outdoor party for his friends and their families. This time of year provided the last chance for such events before the nights became uncomfortably hot in Tucson.

The gathering occurred on an early summer evening with a beautifully calm and clear sky: the perfect night for a garden party. With the help of the Warriors, Tyler lined the walkways, rock walls, and rooftop with luminarias, small brown paper bags partly filled with sand and a lit candle.

They positioned a handful of these lights around the bases of his largest cacti to especially highlight them. Tyler prepared pineapples, watermelons, and other fruits and vegetables for snacks.

Sierra, the families of the Warriors, and some other friends appeared as dusk settled over the desert. The old adobe house and surrounding gardens took on a mysterious look with the winding paths of enchanting luminarias flickering on the cacti. Some guests wandered the scenic paths while others gathered by the food. Everyone patted Beau while he made the rounds in search of affection, missing no chance of a possible caress. Occasionally, he would dart off for some excitement but then quickly return for more love and food.

After eating, Tyler turned off the stereo so that the Warriors and other friends could play their own music. The sounds of fiddles, harmonicas, and guitars floated out over the desert; it seemed as if all the guests played something. People shook maracas and tambourines, others played conga and bongo drums, and some even kept the beat by hitting sticks against logs previously used for seating.

When the music died down, Tyler held a quick meeting with the Warriors' parents about the upcoming Grand Canyon trip. Most of their folks expressed a great deal of concern about the radical occurrences and potential dangers related to following these petroglyph "maps." All felt supportive and eager for their children to enjoy another great summer trip, but they sincerely hoped for no more of these heart-stopping adventures. Tyler tried to ease their minds by detailing the plentiful help available in populated Havasu Canyon and his new insistence on carrying the satellite-activated emergency locator.

The Warriors' families finally concluded that nothing could or ought to prevent their children from following their passions. The young ones' excitement was viral, but beyond making this observation, the adults acknowledged the power of experience.

These parents had learned throughout their own upbringings the benefit of enriching experiences. As kids once left to their own devices, they lived with enough freedom to face, and therefore learn to handle, the many challenges of life on their own. Some of these adults grew up attending European climbing camps, working on friends' ranches, canoeing for days on summertime camp expeditions, or simply traveling independently for sports.

They always came back home to abundant love and support, though each of them had gained an increased sense of confidence and self-reliance while away. This quest clearly filled Tyler and the Warriors with so much wonder and excitement that the parents could only feel grateful that their own children seemed to be really "living" and growing in positive ways.

After the meeting, Tyler invited Sierra up to the roof to catch the first view of the full moon rising over Mica Mountain.

"I hope you can come to the Grand Canyon with us," said Tyler. "The kids would love to have you, and I'm sure their parents would appreciate your presence, too."

"I sure want to join you, and I'm trying to rearrange my work schedule," Sierra replied. "These things tend to work out, but we better get back to our friends before they leave."

It was a fun night, and time seemed to fly by. After the guests had left, Tyler walked with Sierra around the garden paths and extinguished all the candles. They bid each other good night on the back porch in the golden glow of the saguaro ribs, under the watchful eyes of the geckos and elf owls.

With preparations and arrangements settled in the next few weeks, Tyler, Sierra, and the Warriors embarked on the road to the Grand Canyon. In the fiery heat of summer, they eagerly anticipated swimming in the clear turquoise pools below the cascading waterfalls of Havasu Canyon. After passing first through the lower deserts, then the ponderosa, piñon, and juniper forests, and finally the expansive grasslands of the plateau, they came almost unexpectedly upon the famous great, yawning chasm.

"What a shock this must have been to early explorers," announced Colter, for the road abruptly stopped right at the edge of massive cliffs, with an entirely different world way, way down below.

The group of friends pulled into a parking lot bordered by signs pointing toward the start of a trail. This marked path descended into one of the side veins of this great network of canyon arteries. Here they would start their journey deep into the heart of the earth.

Tyler and the Warriors camped at the end of the road and readied their packs for an early start the next morning. One of the many reservation dogs came over and ended up staying the night next to their packs, making the adventurers feel at home.

The trek started at a brisk pace down the steep switchbacks into the chasm as the first rays of dawn lit the sky. Their newfound canine friend, a Labrador mix, led the way. Tyler knew the importance of reaching the creek before the debilitating summer heat overtook them. The switchbacks first descended a white wall of cliffs, but after about an hour of walking, the trail flattened out, and the hikers slowly entered the rising cliffs of the red-walled canyon. Rock and earth now towered above them on both sides, and whenever a cleft in the red wall appeared, one could look up through it at the massive white wall, which now seemed incredibly high above. They ventured deeper into this twisted maze: the heart of the Grand Canyon.

When the group sat on a rock bench for a rest, Sierra spoke up, "The Havasupai sure are fun to visit. I can't wait to see all our friends and catch up on the news."

Tyler and Sierra had journeyed to this wondrous part of the country many times, the Warriors twice. During this momentary pause in their descent, the familiar sights and sounds immediately filled them with joy and contentment. The group took out their water bottles and rehydrated, a habit they practiced consistently at each stop.

"Such an amazing canyon, Havasu," remarked Tyler. "It's the deepest, steepest side canyon in the Grand Canyon. You can easily see it when flying over...Just look at those walls, thousands of feet high!"

As they continued along their route, a rumble echoed through the canyon up ahead, giving way to the sound of steady hoofbeats. Around the bend trotted a string of horses with empty packs strapped to their backs. The Warriors courteously worked their way over to the side of the trail. Bringing up the rear and swinging a lariat approached a tall, stocky Indian with an eagle feather tied to his long black hair. Two dogs followed. He nodded as he rode by on his way to the top, presumably to pick up tourists or feed for his horses.

The adventurers continued descending the dry side canyon until met with the strikingly strong scent of plants and moisture from the larger canyon it began to merge with. Tall trees and lush undergrowth now appeared along the creek that began as a series of small springs just upstream. The always rich turquoise color of the water immediately enticed them to jump in, and the dazzled Warriors floated down the stream, opening their eyes in the crystal-clear water.

They shared the pleasures of flying along with the current and taking in the splendid underwater sights: pure white sand, bright green moss, and emerald-green water plants along the banks, all in brilliant harmony with the turquoise tint of the water.

After this first refreshing swim, they resumed their trek down the now larger canyon. It widened, revealing a hidden paradise flanked by towering red cliffs. The white wall still loomed high above, though farther in the distance. As the group of friends reached the outskirts of the Havasupai village, cornfields and wandering horses surrounded them.

Next, they came upon the board houses that had replaced the old log and brush wikiup lodges of years ago. Here and there, children played in yards, men and women worked their fields, and life continued as many generations had in the past within the quiet depths of the great canyon. Up ahead, molded into the canyon wall near the heart of the village, rose two huge natural rock spires named Wii Gl'iiv. These sacred "Standing Rocks" served as sentinels to the Havasupai domain and provided an awesome sight.

Off the canyon walls echoed the exaggerated sounds of horses stomping, donkeys braying, and voices of men and women calling in the Havasupai language to their children or dogs. Giant cottonwood trees lined the ever-widening path leading into the center of Supai Village. In the front yards of the houses grew lush fruit trees irrigated with water brought directly from the river in dirt canals measuring two or three feet wide.

Around the next bend, a group of unsaddled horses raced toward them, followed by a single smaller horse expertly ridden by a wild and free-looking young boy. A yell of "Horses coming!" arose from the other Havasupais on the trail, and everyone moved to the side to let the stampede pass.

The friendly Labrador proudly escorted the Warriors as they neared the village center and the camping registration office, but he was quickly surrounded and sidetracked by other village dogs. This social mix seemed compatible enough, and no fights broke out among the canines.

With only foot and horse trails available for navigation, no car noises invaded this peaceful canyon. A few days each week, a helicopter would shatter the quiet to bring in supplies or people, but the only sounds heard now came from the locals and their animals starting their day.

After registering for camping, Tyler, Sierra, and the Warriors walked on until the houses disappeared behind them and the creek once again flowed beside the trail. Their guide dog rejoined them with perfect timing; he was long used to picking up tourist groups on the trail and seemed to enjoy the companionship as much as the scraps that came his way. Although many of the local dogs stayed near home, fully loyal to their Havasupai families, others simply chose to run loose for a while before returning home.

The temperature climbed rapidly. Ducking off the trail through the bright green trees and reeds growing thickly along the creek, the youngsters looked for a place to swim. They came upon a beautiful turquoise pool, fully enclosed by the jungle, with a wide ten-foot-high waterfall.

"Come on!" the Warriors shouted to Tyler and Sierra, still back on the trail talking to a horseman.

Meeting at the pool, they all dove in. Everyone thoroughly enjoyed swimming back and forth, diving from the rocks, going deep underwater, resting in the warm shallows, and wiggling their toes in the watercress while tiny fish nibbled at their feet. Surrounded by aquatic life, one felt the possibility of evolving or emerging from the blue-green algae which grew on the bottom of the pool.

The group swam to a tree and climbed up to a platform of branches above the falls to huddle together in the sun. Makoa stayed in the water, floating peacefully on his back while holding onto a slender tree branch.

Tyler spotted some movement in the brush; a dark-skinned, bare-chested boy appeared. With raven-black hair flowing down his back, he wore the look of a native canyon dweller of the distant past.

A few more local kids appeared behind him, walking barefoot but smoothly on the rough coral-like rocks. The lab barked at first, but soon settled down in the bushes.

While Sierra returned to the packs to make peanut butter sandwiches, Tyler and the Warriors watched from the "tree fort" as the Havasupai boys and girls took turns diving off the waterfall. These "people of the blue-green water" appeared totally at home in the water, diving gracefully and swimming as smoothly as dolphins. The children looked up and waved in a friendly manner, inviting The Warriors to jump from the platform and swim over to meet them. The native kids then took them on a tour of the pool's best diving spots.

They played a version of follow the leader, each one diving from different rock ledges or tree branches. Tyler dove in to sit on a rock at the water's edge and watch while the Warriors played with the Havasupais, exploring along the bank. Swimming under submerged tree trunks like a school of curious fish, they made their way beneath a veil of grape vines and branches to a hidden part of the pool with its own little waterfall. Tyler swam to catch up.

After another hour of swimming, eating, and exploring together, they quickly became friends. The Havasupai kids asked Tyler, Sierra, and the Warriors to join them with their fathers and uncles at the sweat lodge the following day.

"We'd be honored," Tyler responded.

The native children looked at each other and uttered, "Ma," meaning "go" in their language, then disappeared into the brush. A few minutes later, they could be seen on the embankment above the trees riding back to the village atop colorful blankets on bareback ponies.

"I wish I could live like these kids do: riding, hiking, and swimming all the time," Shawnee said dreamily.

After one more dip into the water, the explorers lifted their packs and continued down the trail. Their volunteer watchdog, known to the locals as Bear-Bear, roused himself from his nap and crawled out of the bushes to join them. They neared Navajo Falls, the first major waterfall along this route that issued from a dense green forest covering the entire cliff face, and decided for now not to explore it; there would be time for that later.

They stopped next at the top of the towering Havasu Falls and savored the view of this most idyllic scene. The large pool at the bottom took on various shades of turquoise. Water flowed out into several small, picturesque travertine dammed pools below, creating a series of bubbling "Jacuzzis." Giant cottonwoods and cattail reeds grew along the banks. The waterfall, a huge and powerful white cascade that dropped 100 feet from a red cliff of bizarre "dripping" rock beside a curtain of green moss, already captured the attention of a scattering of Havasupais and tourists.

Young men and kids swung from a long rope that hung from one of the giant trees, and the Warriors could not wait to join them. Tyler's group hurried past the falls to the campground, eager to lose their packs and get back for the fun. Sierra decided to stay, set up camp, and join them again momentarily.

With the fierce heat of the afternoon sun upon them, the adventurers returned to the waterfall and swam to their hearts' content. Like fish, they paddled first against the current, then turned to go with the flow, and repeatedly dove into the depths of the crystal-clear turquoise water. Before long, Sierra joined them in the beautiful pools among the rock formations. Together they swam behind the falls into a hurricane-like mist, climbed out onto some rocks and dove out the other side, took turns at the rope swing, and explored the fern grottos lining the cliff underneath the falls.

By the time the sun had set behind the white wall to the west, they felt completely exhausted and ready to make camp. As night fell on the great canyon, its highest white walls to the east turned golden in the last fading rays of daylight. The lower canyon had already fallen into darkness, producing a contrast that highlighted the radical relief of this rugged land. Eventually, all the walls turned black, beneath a strip of dark blue sky studded with glittering stars that burned with intense clarity.

Tyler and his crew lay in their bags before drifting off to sleep, feeling in their souls the canyon's awesome depth and remoteness. Nestled within the canyon walls, they could hear the waterfalls echoing in the background. All of the hiking and swimming had prepared the group for a full night of sound rest

While his body recharged overnight, Makoa dreamed that he could swim underwater without coming up for air. Colter hit home runs over a canyon wall in his sleep. Shawnee dreamed of riding a beautiful horse down steep, narrow canyon trails until coming to a waterfall. She took her horse behind the falls until they were totally hidden and protected by the water. The horse suddenly transformed into a water spirit and evaporated into the sky. Shawnee wondered if she would evaporate next, but instead awoke, very moved by her dream. She wished desperately to be riding freely on a horse again.

Having slept soundly, everyone greeted the day in good spirits. Today, they would explore more of this land of the blue-green waters and only carry daypacks.

After taking one more quick dip into Havasu Falls, Tyler, Sierra, and the Warriors packed lunch for the afternoon and began meandering back upstream. This time, they did stop at Navajo Falls: a high, tumbling waterfall with an emerald-green hanging forest dropping down beside it. The steep escarpment, which measured about 100 yards high, housed many small caves with water running out of them.

After swimming for a bit, they ate lunch together on a big log near the main pool. The Warriors completely packed away any trash accumulated during their meal and proceeded to climb up to the fern-wreathed caves. Encrusted by the mineral-rich water, the exposed roots within these caverns had turned into intricate stone stalactites over time. They traversed over to a good diving ledge, and each of them performed a jump or swan dive into an area of the pool already extensively checked for adequate depth. (The Havasupai Tourist office now emphasizes safety and therefore advises against all diving because of many unfortunate accidents.) The time to reconvene with their Havasupai friends up at the sweat lodge quickly drew near, so they resumed the hike up canyon.

As the explorers approached the earth-covered mound by the creek, they could see a large fire tended by several Havasupai males; the men's long black hair hung loosely, and they wore only shorts. The native youngsters that the Warriors had befriended the previous day greeted the visitors and introduced their fathers and uncles. One man lifted several stones from the middle of the coals with a pitchfork and placed them into the sweat lodge. Next, in groups of four to five, everyone took turns sweating while Bear-Bear waited outside.

The Havasupai hosts explained, "The sweat lodge represents the womb of Mother Earth, our original mother, in a sense. We enter going backwards. The last one in pulls the blanket over the door. When you come out facing forward, it symbolizes 'rebirth' or a fresh start."

One of the elders chanted and said prayers, mostly in the native tongue but with some parts in English for the benefit of his guests. He prayed for health and well-being for all, including the Earth and the great-grandmother canyon, their home. Then he sang in Havasupai while throwing handfuls of water from a bucket onto the hissing rocks.

He turned toward Tyler's group and said, "The spirits of the rocks are talking. Everything in nature has a spirit that we should honor and respect."

A cloud of steam rose, engulfing them in hot vapor, and thus began the ritual bonding between humankind and the spiritual power of the earth. The extremely hot sweat lodge caused perspiration to run freely from their bodies. The Warriors bravely endured as the Havasupai man leading the ceremony sang his four songs. Some of the participants lowered their heads near the ground to escape the hottest upper level of air; others blew their own breath on sore muscles or joints to increase the heat and healing to those areas. After the four songs ended, everyone emerged to wander off into the creek.

Before heading home, the father of one of the Havasupai youth invited their new friends over to see their spring colts. Tyler, Sierra, and the Warriors followed him through the village to his abode, where they encountered all the uncles, aunts, and other family members sitting around an outside table. The kids eagerly led a few frisky young horses around the yard as the surrounding cliffs glowed brightly with the approaching sunset.

A Havasupai uncle pointed out various rock formations looming above them. "There's Wii Baa'a, the Man of Stone, and Wii Gl'iiv... and look, bighorn sheep high up on the cliffs! I haven't seen them in a while. They're now federally protected, though we once hunted them at certain ceremonial times.

Makoa politely added, "Bighorns happen to be one of my favorite animals."

"Ours, too," the native man responded. "The Guardians of the Grand Canyon perform dances with ram horns on their heads. They are a ceremonial group that now honors the bighorns as well as the canyon. Have you seen them before?"

Tyler described seeing one such performance at the Grand Canyon Village, located up on the South Rim.

One of the wise grandfathers belonging to this family jumped in to share a brief history with the interested guests.

He began, "The Havasupai people left archeological evidence dating back 700 years or so, though we feel we have been in the area much longer. Past generations lived on the southern rim of the Grand Canyon, and our ancestral land stretched east, to the San Francisco Peaks and beyond, toward the realm of our traditional friends the Hopis. We Havasupai speak a Hokan language and apparently descend from the first people to migrate from Asia over the Bering Land Bridge about 30,000 years ago. Our Hopi neighbors continue to carry on the ancestral ceremonies.

"Archeologists have different theories of our particular tribe's origins. We are potentially descendants of an Anasazi group, now referred to as Ancestral Puebloans, or might come from displaced people who lived south of here, generally called the Cohonina. One other possible lineage of the Havasupai is from a culture previously located in West-Central Arizona called the Cerbat, a Yuman group. The Hopi currently residing to our east are believed to have come from the prehistoric Ancestral Puebloan culture, as well. Anthropologists claim that our two cultures converged at the Grand Canyon around 1300 AD. The first evidence of that ancient Puebloan culture in the canyon dates back to 500 AD."

"Red Hawk," the host politely interrupted, "take your friends to help bring in the horses. Give them what's left of the feed. I'm going up tomorrow."

The white-haired Havasupai man continued, "The San Francisco Peaks near Flagstaff lie between the lands of the Hopi tribe and ours, and these mountains are considered the home of the kachinas or ancestral spirits. Navajo people living mostly to the north and east also hold these peaks as a sacred natural place.

"The Hopi believe their ancestors emerged into the world alongside the turquoise-blue waters of the Little Colorado, another large side canyon within the Grand Canyon. Along its banks there is a dome built up from the mineral content of the water that bubbles to the surface; this is allegedly the precise location of Hopi emergence.

"The Havasupai have lived both within the canyon among the rocks and above it, on or near the rim. In the past, Havasupais spent summers on the canyon floor growing crops. Then we would move to the top of the canyon in the winter and melt snow for water because there are no streams, and we would hunt mainly elk and deer for meat and hides. Red Butte, south of here, served as our spiritual landmark and the center of our territory. The red cliffs enclosing our village are called the Supai Group by geologists; they even named three of the rock layers within the Supai Group after three of our traditional family surnames."

The Havasupais told a few more stories until it was time for Tyler, Sierra, and the Warriors to go back to camp. A strip of stars shone brightly above, leading them home between the black canyon walls. Bear-Bear trotted in front with renewed energy from the cool night air. After arriving at their site, they fixed something to eat and bedded down for the night.

The Warriors awoke early the next day to the wonderful sounds of the canyon, ate breakfast, and readied their packs for a trip farther down canyon to the area that seemed to be marked with the arrowhead on the petroglyph.

Tyler went over plans with Sierra, "We will camp just past the Havasupai Reservation, on the Grand Canyon National Park side, which is halfway from here to the Colorado River. We were lucky to get a special permit for one night."

Sierra interrupted, "I've decided to stay at camp while you guys search. Someone needs to hold down the fort." Tyler assented to her decision, and they readily agreed on a plan. Sierra would go with the others only as far as Mooney Falls.

Before long, they set out and came to the top of the 200-foot waterfall, the highest in the canyon. Bear-Bear lay down in the cool shade of a cave. He understood that he could go no farther and would either wait or wander back to the campground or village.

"He sure seems to know what's going on," laughed Sierra.

The trail descended, for the most part vertically, to the side of the falls through a series of caves and steep steps cut into and through the rock. The Warriors, while descending the cliff and looking out from the various opened caves, took pictures of the beautiful pool at the base of the cascade. This deeper pool possessed an even darker and richer shade of blue than the pool at Havasu Falls, except for the shallows which shimmered in lighter shades of turquoise. Small waves rolled out steadily from the base of Mooney Falls as the falling water battered the surface with a loud thunder and a hurricane of spray. The gigantic walls were decorated with curtains and canopies of rock, formed from the mineral-rich water flowing over in different places throughout the years.

After surveying the scene and planning where to explore, the group climbed down the cliff, eager to start swimming in the magnificent pool. They waded across a shallow travertine dam and dropped their packs on some land in the middle of the stream. Lush plants grew thickly on the little island, including horse-tailed reeds, descendants of tree ferns that lived millions of years ago.

Back at the pool, Tyler and Sierra dove in first and swam underwater along a trail of white sand bordered by tall, waving bright green seaweed. Happily kicking like dolphins, they found themselves going deeper toward the dark-blue depths. They eventually surfaced in the middle of the pool to gaze at the water falling in large white sheets. Next, Makoa led the Warriors, jumping from a rock jutting out and into the pool. With his Hawaiian heritage, Makoa seemed especially confident and "at one" in this blue-water world. The friends explored all areas of the giant pool: more ledges to jump from, caves behind the falls, and other deep spots to venture into.

After the swim, they came back to their packs and rested in the sun. Tyler glanced up at the towering walls, and for some reason, his eye was curiously drawn to two men at the top of the waterfall: one white, with a floppy hat and binoculars, and another who appeared to be a Havasupai. The dark-skinned man seemed relaxed as he looked out over the canyon, but the tall, scrawny white guy with the big hat looked agitated, ill at ease, and unusually interested in the humans down below. He seemed to be specifically focused on Tyler's group and directed the other man's gaze toward them.

Tyler felt uneasy and slipped behind a tree for cover. Peeking through the branches at these men high above while thinking to himself that he must be getting paranoid, he heeded the uncomfortable feeling and decided it was time to go. He and the three Warriors said their goodbyes to Sierra, put their packs on, and started down the trail beside the creek, still under the watchful eye of the men above the falls. Tyler knew that fear depends on instinct more than reason and could not help but carry on wondering.

Tyler and his young friends followed the narrow path through heavy jungle-like vegetation, briskly turned a corner, and were hidden at last by the canyon walls. Colter needed a bathroom break, so the others waited as he ran to the base of the cliff and dug a hole. All of them knew the best bathroom practices for the environment while spending time in nature: to dig a hole about six inches deep and away from any water, and to burn toilet paper only if it was safe to do so. They could always pack out any used paper in a plastic bag to be thrown in the trash later. They soon continued down the canyon again, stopping often to swim in the beckoning pools.

As they walked along the creek lined with vines and trees, Tyler noticed a bright snake with black and white stripes slithering across the bank. The large California kingsnake moved excitedly to the edge of a rock, arched like a coiled spring, and launched itself down. Knowing that the snake must be hunting, Tyler crept up to the rock and peered over. He spotted a smaller sand-colored Grand Canyon rattlesnake constricted within the tight coils of its hunter while its little rattle still shook slowly from side to side. The Warriors came over to see.

"Wow, that is cool! I've finally seen it, a kingsnake eating a rattlesnake," said Makoa, as the rattlesnake slowly slid down whole into the larger snake's mouth.

Not long after witnessing this spectacle, the adventurers came to a deep, large pool and dove in for a game of underwater tag. The Warriors swam as fluidly as the water itself under deep sunken logs and through pillars of roots encrusted like coral by the water's minerals. Tired from their game, they rested on thrones of moss below a series of small waterfalls. Before long, it was time to pack up and continue hiking downstream. Wild grape vines and shoulder-high grasses crowded the trail. Tyler pointed out two sturdy desert bighorn rams off to the side, their curled horns sticking up above the vines.

By the afternoon, the friends had reached a 40-foot waterfall. Just past this would be the dry narrow side canyon that seemed to be the one marked on the petroglyph map! Here, the inner cliffs rose many hundreds of feet on either side, and two more tiers of cliffs and talus existed above those; at this point, the Warriors were situated a mile deep in the earth. They vigorously scouted the walls at the junction and saw many caves, searching those that were accessible before eventually going back below the falls to one of the larger pools to swim and rest.

While they lay nestled in the tall grass, multicolored dragonflies zipped back and forth over the pool in front of them, catching smaller flying insects.

Makoa, a student of ancient creatures, asked, "Did you guys know that in the Carboniferous Period of the Paleozoic Era, dragonflies had three-foot wingspans?"

Too tired to answer, the others sat mesmerized, wondering where the cave might be and watching the dragonflies going back and forth.

"A goddess of water must surely live here," said Tyler, feeling the beauty of the place working its magic. “I could watch the constant motion of water with its ever-changing textures for hours." He dropped his chin onto the top of his fist to further study the whirling waters.

“It’s like listening to the flow of time,” Makoa said thoughtfully. “Maybe we're naturally drawn to water because our bodies are mostly water. Our life depends so much on this precious liquid.”

“Or maybe our love of water is because life seems to have evolved from water,” pondered Shawnee.

"I'm still scared to swim to the bottom of those deep, dark holes below the falls," admitted Colter. “At night, I can scare myself by sitting near a river and thinking it is bewitched, a writhing serpent full of eerie sounds, voices, and music.”

“That’s a perfect example of how one’s mind, with fear mixed in, can really play tricks on you,” Tyler commented. “The flowing sounds of water are generally thought to be an age-old tranquilizer. And with time on its side, water can cut through mountains of solid stone on its journey downward via the path of least resistance. Its persistence gives it incredible strength."

"Okay, but where do you think the cave is?" asked Colter, revealing his persistence.

"Well," Tyler said, "the map has it marked in a side canyon, and this side canyon is the only one in this part of the canyon."

"But we've looked everywhere!" said Makoa. "Where else can it be?"

"If this cave is as hard to find as the others, it could still be here somewhere," said Shawnee.

The Warriors faced another challenge beyond finding the cave, for the scrawny man who had watched them earlier from the cliff top was none other than the conniving Dr. Shaw. From Tyler's sleep-talking clues, it wasn't hard for the doctor to figure out the secret of the eagle petroglyph map that he had also copied from the cave. The obvious lines depicting the Grand Canyon and Havasu Canyon had led him all the way to the side canyon, and he had already spent two days searching high and low for the cave – with no luck.

Knowing that only a small window of time remained to explore the canyon before the monsoon season of possible flash floods, Dr. Shaw also recognized the chance of running into Tyler. Trying to minimize his risk of seeing Tyler in the lower canyon, Shaw had gone back to the campground each evening. Now he decided to keep a closer eye on the adventurers and let them find this other cave for him. With their full packs on, they were obviously heading down canyon to camp. For now, the doctor would have to settle for not having first dibs at whatever treasures might lie in such a cave, but he knew from the last time that Tyler and the Warriors seemed to leave everything.

Having anticipated the possibility of being seen, Dr. Shaw cut his beard, wore a big droopy hat and sunglasses, and spread white zinc oxide on his face as sunscreen: a disguise meant to blend in with other tourists. If the group recognized him, he could still act like it was a coincidence. He needed to somehow spy on them in order to succeed in locating the cave.

Afraid of stumbling into the group, he offered to pay a Havasupai acquaintance, the man who had packed him down to the campground, to help find Tyler's camp within the canyon. Shaw then planned to cautiously approach their location and keep watch from a hiding spot, as he'd done before. He fabricated a story, telling the packer that Shawnee was his daughter. The doctor claimed that he wanted to eventually catch up to her, surprise her, and drive her home at the end of the trip. He explained his concern about losing track of them and wanted to be close by if she became injured or homesick. At the same time, he insisted that he didn't want to interfere with her trip until the last day.

The Havasupai man generously gave his help for free; he wanted to visit that part of the canyon anyway and do some fishing.

By late afternoon, Tyler and the Warriors started searching for a place to camp. Just downstream from the 40-foot waterfall, they found a large rock with a huge grape vine draped over it, forming a sort of hut – a perfect spot for the night. After unpacking some essentials, they stretched out and relaxed on the soft, sandy ground in the shade of the vines. Tyler found a layer of pure white powdery lime in the nearby cliff and started a sand painting to pass the time before making dinner.

The main trail that led down the canyon ran above them. The group could not be seen, but there was one ledge where a hiker might potentially spot their camp. Although engaged in his artwork, Tyler picked up some movement from the corner of his eye. He didn't get a good look, only saw something dark, and dismissed it as a low-flying raven or the shadow of a hawk. In reality, the Havasupai scout had just discovered their camp; his long, black hair flowed behind like a raven's wing as he instantly passed from view.

The shadows darkened, and the adventurers sat together, talking and cooking dinner on their camp stoves. Large, fragrant white datura flowers started to open for the night. Soon it would be dark, and they could feel the canyon brimming with life as the day creatures sang their last songs and the night animals and insects began theirs. At this hour, the tree frogs filled the canyon with a sweet symphony.

The Warriors set out their sleeping bags and looked up past the steep black walls to spot their favorite summer constellation, Scorpio, before dozing off to sleep. Everyone slept soundly with the creek sounds filling their dreams.

After he spotted Tyler's group, the Havasupai man hiked toward home on the jungle-like trail below Mooney Falls while darkness descended on the canyon. He turned on his small flashlight to avoid rattlesnakes on this warm summer evening. Suddenly, he heard a large animal, apparently startled off the trail and bounding into the bushes ahead of him. As he came around the next bend and peered into the thicket, his flashlight revealed two huge golden eyes reflecting back. A deep, throaty growl sent the Indian running up the trail.

Arriving at Dr. Shaw's tent covered with sweat, the Havasupai reported on the whereabouts of Tyler and the Warriors. He said nothing to the doctor about the giant glowing eyes but immediately went back to the village to tell his friends about the big mountain lion, very likely hunting bighorn in the lower canyon. Shaw made plans to hike down-canyon the following day, satisfied that now he had a better chance of approaching the group without being seen.

The Warriors woke early to again search the side canyon for the Indian cave: still no luck. After enjoying lunch at camp, they went to the pool beneath the falls for a swim. Makoa waded out to a mushroom-shaped rock sticking out of the water, stood on top of it, and dove in. He shot across to a deep bay off to the side of the main current. From there, a rapidly moving back eddy bore him upstream along an overhanging wall of ferns toward the waterfall. Approaching the falls, he dove deeply under the bubbles and spotted a colorful rainbow trout. The fish darted toward deeper water, but Makoa chased it down before pushing off the bottom into the faster current at the surface. He then drifted downstream on his back, in awe of the canyon's towering walls.

Colter, Shawnee, and Tyler followed their friend, jumping into the deep back eddy and swimming like otters. Makoa climbed out onto the bank and walked back upstream to do it all over again. After hearing about the huge trout, the other Warriors swam toward the deeper parts of the pool to look for more.

Tyler retrieved his goggles before going back to look for fish in the sunlit pool. As he slipped in, a large rainbow trout streaked by him, swimming deeper to get away. Tyler had enough breath left to follow and chased the fish into the clear blue depths.

A dark object moving along the bottom toward the waterfall caught his eye. Its large, flat tail was unmistakable; the beaver swam straight into a dark hole within the rock under the waterfall and disappeared.

Forced to surface for a breath, Tyler told the others, "There's a beaver tunnel under the falls! I saw one go into it. I'm going to get the flashlight and have a look."

He returned to the pool with the waterproof light hanging on a lanyard around his neck. Diving from the rocks above the cave, he used momentum to shoot down 10 feet toward his target like an arrow. Thankfully, the sun shone fully on the pool, and the visibility was good. With the anticipation of possibly finding baby beavers in their nest, Tyler ventured into the hole and up a sloping tunnel. Just as his air started running out, he saw a "mirrored" surface above him, instead of rock. Drawing from past experience that this visual indicated an air space, he stretched his hands out for protection and popped his head up, hoping to find enough room to breathe.

Seconds later, Tyler found himself above water level in a chamber dimly lit by sunlight from the pool. He edged over to a ledge and sat for a moment. Sparkling droplets fell from several stalactites surrounding him, filling the room with an eerie echo having many different tones. What a mysterious cave tucked up under the waterfall Tyler had encountered! He got up to explore, first passing through a frigid dripping curtain of water.

"I guess you've got to go through the chills to get the thrills..." he said to himself as he toughened up against the cold. Before him stood a group of four light-turquoise stalagmites, about three feet tall. A drip fell periodically onto each one with a delicate splash from a stalactite directly above.

Tyler walked into the middle of the formations, positively stunned. As he examined them more closely, he noticed crystal clear arrowheads embedded near the top of each stalagmite. Could this be the Indian cave? He could hardly believe his luck. After looking around briefly to further admire the decorative cave formations, then remembering the Warriors who might worry at his disappearance, he swam out to share his discovery and bring them in.

Girl in Falls

Leif Jones, Havasupai

Ram

Matthew Putsoy, Havasupai

Teratorn
Pete Connolly

7

Ancient Magic

The Guide
An ageless man gave a gift to me
He showed me the wonders of the land
Opened my mind so I could see,
Helping me grow and understand.

He had eyes that glowed from a weathered face
unmarred by lines of care
I remember him still as the breeze whipped softly
through his wavy, wind-blown hair

Though I was only a child,
on many adventures we went
I grew to love the wild
In my heart a thrill was sent.

We climbed the mountains
and drank the crystal air,
swam in the clear blue fountains,
and hardly had a care.

We watched clouds form in the sky
and shared our hopes and dreams,
Watched eagles soar and fly
and heard their savage screams.

We explored caves down below
With formations white as snow,
learned about the earth,
and how much there was to know.

Then one day he went away.
I really don't know where.
So I sat by the fire in silence,
more lonely than I could bear.

I thought back over the places we'd been
and the things that we had shared,
until I saw him in my memory
with his wavy, windblown hair.

I remembered that first day we met
and the gift he spoke of.
I smiled to myself as I realized
that the gift given was

Love of mighty places,
of solitude and light,
of thunderous, raging rivers
and storm-filled summer nights.

As I walked through a desert canyon
amid dizzying rock-face heights,
I came to a large cascade

falling from incredibly beautiful sights.

When I knelt to drink from the pool below
my reflection made me start,
for gazing back from the mirrored surface
was a wise man with an ageless heart.

With eyes that glowed from a weathered face
unmarred by lines of care,
and the breeze was whipping softly
through my wavy, windblown hair.

Hidden among campfire memories
And a thousand tongues of flame
Remembering exploration and adventure
That stimulated muscle and brain

Happiness is never in the future.
It is in what is and what has been.
The story of a man is told
not in the pages of a ledger,
but in the lines that crease his face and hands,
and in the depth of his eyes.
--Anonymous (Reworked by Author)

It was a great relief when Tyler reappeared after apparently being underwater for so long. When he told of his find, the Warriors hooted with joy and begged to see the cave. They followed Tyler to the edge of the waterfall, dove in single file beneath the falls, and came up through the tunnel.

Once reunited in the cave, the explorers gathered, awestruck, in the circle of arrowheads and dripping stalactites. Though chattering from the cold, no one felt in any hurry to leave.

Tyler had already looked around and knew that no other passages led away from the room, aside from another small hole below water level right beside the one through which they had popped up. While the others examined the arrowheads, he went back to the water-filled tunnel. He knelt down beside the other small, submerged hole and cautiously reached the length of his arm inside to see if it might be a possible passage.

Tyler turned to his young friends. "I'm going to check out this little tunnel to see if it goes anywhere."

With his goggles on and waterproof flashlight in hand, he took a big breath, submerged, and crawled into the body-sized tube, working his way through it like a worm. He started running out of breath and thought about backing out but saw just beyond him the familiar mirrored surface. He went for it, popping up into an air hole only about one square foot in area – certainly not much space, but enough for him to take a steadying breath or two before continuing.

Forever the explorer, Tyler wormed his way on and found another smaller breathing hole. This time, he had to turn his head since the jagged air pocket was only inches above the water. He took a panicked breath and decided to go forward one more stretch.

Tyler felt the claustrophobia building and recognized that if he did not find a spot wide enough to turn around, he would have a difficult time wiggling out backwards. Encountering sticks and driftwood soon made his progress even more challenging. Another breathing hole appeared; he stuck his head up and, finally, found room.

Tyler's adrenaline subsided while his senses adjusted to new surroundings: a small space that housed a mass of shaved sticks and a strong animal smell. His eyes focused on some branches overflowing from a side nook, and then he heard a slight rustle. Crawling over and peering slowly into the jumble of sticks revealed four curled up baby beavers. Another very narrow tunnel near the nest led down into the water and directly out to the pool. Mistaking the intruder for their mother, the babies began to whine. Tyler tried to reassure them with his own whimpering sounds until all fell quiet.

One of the corners with a very low roof was choked with small stalactites, stained dark red, hanging down eight inches or so and similar stalagmites rising up to meet them. Together, the two groups of formations appeared like teeth. Amongst the "teeth," two eyes stared at him.

Tyler looked harder – utterly shocked – and reached back in among the formations to gently retrieve a ten-inch carved rock jaguar. Mostly made of green jade, the figurine was dotted with yellow golden spots encircled by black lava rock. The little jaguar had eyes of amber.

Tyler quickly examined it, then looked around the area more thoroughly but found nothing else. Looking once more at the cute sleeping beavers, he held the carving carefully in front of him in disbelief and slithered anxiously back through the tunnel to his friends. The jade jaguar emerged first, followed by Tyler, gasping for breath. The Warriors felt overwhelmed by the discovery, thinking this could be the end of their long quest. However, they would soon find out that fate had not quite finished with them yet.

Makoa, Colter, and Shawnee took turns examining the carving, jostling for a closer look as Tyler made a tiny test scratch to verify the metallic spots as real gold. Shawnee called attention to some faint lines etched on the underside of the figurine.

This hand-crafted design included two exploding volcanoes with a flat-topped pyramid between them. A stylized Mayan jaguar face appeared on one side of the pyramid. Included in the scene was none other than Kokopelli, as well as the same lizard symbol seen at the other caves.

Around the edges, the artist had included shapes that looked like bats, also in the style of the ancient Maya.

"I wonder where this map leads," said Makoa. "There aren't any arrowheads marking anything like before."

"You know what?" Tyler realized, "These lines look like the Baja California peninsula. Here's the main Mexican coast and, the volcanoes and pyramid are in southern Maya country."

"The Kokopelli and lizard are on a hump of some sort near the coast, between what looks like two volcanoes," observed Shawnee.

Colter offered, "Maybe they're petroglyphs on a large rock or cliff."

"And this winding line leading between the volcanoes could represent a river going inland," added Makoa. "Look – here's a dotted line that connects it to the jaguar pyramid."

"It's awfully faint; it may be another overland trail," said Tyler. "Let's take our find outside to see it in the sunlight. We'll bring it back after taking a photograph. I think we've found a Mayan artifact brought up from the jungles of Central America."

Everyone swam out of the cave, and Tyler held tightly onto the carved jaguar. As they approached their packs, some ravens flew off.

One had apparently learned to loosen zippers, evidenced by some nuts and dried fruits found scattered about. Munching on the remainder of these snacks, the Warriors settled into a comfortable grassy "nest" and passed the jaguar carving around. A collective sigh expressed their awe. In the sunlight the gold glimmered and the amber eyes glowed.

Following the flash of those glittering golden eyes, a man's head slowly protruded from a clump of bushes tucked under the cliff a short distance above the group. If Tyler and the Warriors had not been so engrossed in their discovery, they might have noticed another tell-tale flash from Dr. Shaw's binoculars as he just spotted them from the higher trail. The sight of this obvious treasure quickened his heartbeat while he focused.

Something more like wine than blood began to flow through his veins as a greedy lust overcame him. Feeling upset that he had not discovered the cave entrance that had produced the gold studded carving, he now felt at least a slim chance of obtaining the treasure. While Shaw struggled with these thoughts, a feeling gripped his stomach, telling him that he was heading down the path of his own destruction.

The young Warriors spread out their towels for an afternoon rest and dozed off on the comfortable grass, but Tyler felt too excited to sleep. He tried to lie still and study the jaguar perched on his stomach. Unable to contain his restlessness, he picked up his throwing knife and the carving and walked along the edge of the pool. Looking for a dead tree trunk or clay bank to use for a little knife-throwing practice, he followed a small path up to a ledge overlooking some larger pools. He sat down to analyze the carving again.

Dr. Shaw happened to have situated himself in the rocks just above Tyler's position and now watched his every move. There, right in front of the doctor, was the priceless object he so desired. A cold, evil feeling like a frozen dagger entered his heart, carved its way to his mind, and developed into a plan. He became mesmerized by the ancient carving and utterly hypnotized by greed.

Shielded by a large rock and some brush, Dr. Shaw lurked quite close to Tyler. Feeling coldly detached, as if icy water trickled down his spine, Shaw acted on a sudden bold idea and stepped from behind the rock – holding a pistol. He looked disconnected, unsure; the gun wavered as if it had a life of its own.

Tyler heard the swish of bushes and briskly turned around, speechless at the sight of Dr. Shaw pointing a gun at him. He could hardly begin to comprehend this moment.

As Tyler struggled to understand, bearing the expression of one straining to see through smoke, he erupted, "Stop! Dr. Shaw! What are you doing? What's wrong?"

Shaw pointed a stiff skeleton-like finger at the figurine. "Where did you find that?" he demanded with rising intensity, ignoring the other man's questions.

Tyler answered, "I brought this with me from home to leave as a sort of offering."

"Is that right? Are you sure you didn't find that down here?"

"Dr. Shaw, what are you doing? How'd you know about this? Have you been following us?"

"You're a good sleep-talker under the effects of rattlesnake venom."

"Please..." urged Tyler. "Why would you throw your life away by doing something like this?"

Dr. Shaw's beady red eyes and beak-like nose gave him the appearance of a vulture. Seemingly having gone off the "deep end," he looked right through Tyler.

"I'm not throwing anything away because I don't plan on getting caught. Besides, I owe you some payback! Remember the man you once helped the Game and Fish Department arrest for poaching that jaguar? Your butting into my affairs cost me dearly."

It then dawned on Tyler, as if the sun had just burst through the clouds, that Shaw was the same man he had seen years ago hunting in a remote area of southern Arizona. His mind's eye flooded with events from the past. Due to his position high on a hill at the time, Tyler couldn't tell exactly what fell victim to the hunter in the heavy brush. From many loud reports of a large-caliber gun and the hunter's apparent caution and excitement, it appeared to be big game. Later on, Tyler had run into a Game and Fish officer on the road and described what he'd seen because it was not hunting season. The officer followed the lead and found that the hunter had unbelievably killed a jaguar, a protected, endangered species. This led to an arrest and a conviction, followed by a large fine and jail time for the offender.

When he got out of jail, the poacher had changed his name to his wife's: from Dr. Harvey Pew to Dr. Harvey Shaw. The extensive bad press ruined his medical practice, forcing him to start over in Tucson under his new name. Part of his parole included working rescues and other community service jobs. Tyler never saw a photo of the poacher, but Pew recalled seeing Tyler's name on the Game and Fish report supplied to him by his lawyer.

Cursing like a spitting wild cat, Shaw yelled, “Give it to me or I’ll shoot!” His veins pulsed as though moles burrowed around his temples. He tried desperately to decide what to do, and the final decision shot like a bullet through his brain. To not waste any more time, the doctor would just take the priceless carving and force Tyler off the cliff, making it look like an accident.

"Give me that carving," Shaw demanded again, "or you'll feel the burn of this hot lead!” He waved the gun around dangerously; his eyes glazed over like those of a madman.

Tyler stared at him with a steady, piercing glare, as if looking through the bore of a leveled rifle.

He began to plead, “Dr. Shaw, please, I didn’t know who it was. I only wanted to protect our wildlife. Don’t do this!” Tyler paused to take a deep breath and said, “Here, you can have the carving.”

He held out the carving as Shaw cocked back the hammer of his pistol. The doctor’s crazed eyes clearly revealed his deadly intention.

Tyler stood strong and stared right into the doctor's eyes, grappling with his soul. But Dr. Shaw had gone too far. Tyler hesitated for an instant before seizing on a desperate plan. His eyes darkened, and he steeled himself for battle as electric messages of danger hummed through his body.

Feeling a surge of adrenaline, Tyler held out the carving with one hand while scrambling with the other to find the throwing knife hidden in the waistband of his shorts. It took but an instant to adjust the knife in his hand and let it fly.

Upon seeing the flash of steel, Dr. Shaw fired his gun. Amazingly, the bullet hit the knife in midair and deflected it over the cliff. Both men stood stunned for an instant. Tyler seized his opportunity to lunge in and grab the revolver from Shaw’s hand, like a bald eagle plucking fish from still water. Sadly, he couldn't hold onto it. The gun flew through the air and landed on the other side of a jumble of large rocks.

Awakened by the shot, the Warriors instantly noticed that Tyler wasn't in camp and started cautiously down the path.

As Shaw sprinted toward the gun, Tyler decided to take a chance. The weapon had fallen closer to the doctor, and Tyler knew that in order to get to it first, he would have to cut across the pile of rocks and grape vines blocking his shortest route. He leapt across the boulders with long, powerful strides that shot him through the air as if gravity failed to exist. The seasoned outdoorsman negotiated the vines, but a rock suddenly rolled out from under him, and he slammed into the ground.

Recovering with the quickness of a cat, Tyler sprang to his feet, but once again faced the mouth of the gun. With the pistol leveled at his enemy, Dr. Shaw slowly walked over and picked up the jade carving dropped during the scuffle. He maneuvered and threatened Tyler to the very edge of the cliff, then hesitated.

Dr. Shaw knew there was no turning back. He had to get rid of Tyler and escape before he risked being seen. He figured that the only way to get Tyler off the cliff was to shoot him.

As he cocked the hammer back, he heard a rustle in the bushes behind him, followed by a deep and powerful growl. The depth of danger conveyed by this threatening sound froze both men in place. The bushes suddenly parted, revealing the spotted head and shoulders of a jaguar. Tyler instantly recognized his pal!

Dr. Shaw turned to fire at the beast, but Jag had already launched into the air. The huge cat slammed him to the ground and slashed repeatedly with his giant lethal claws. The Warriors burst upon the scene and watched in horror as the jaguar gripped the doctor's shoulder with his mighty jaws and dragged him to the cliff's edge. Jag's savage growls, even though muffled with the man in his mouth, were amplified to a level of intensity utterly hard to believe.

Shaw twisted and clawed at the ground frantically as the big cat's dagger-like teeth worked toward the head, piercing his face and skull. Jag abruptly released his grip and dropped his prey with a hideous snarl. The bloody, hysterical man hit the ground. With eyes bulging from their sockets and in a mad effort to get away, the doctor went over the cliff. A terrifying scream sounded as the onlookers heard tree branches breaking, followed by a final thud.

Tyler and the Warriors looked with wide eyes at Jag. They all recalled the unique markings on the cat's face and wondered how on earth their friend could be here, so far from where they had left him. Momentarily looking "into" the familiar humans, his large golden eyes glowed with deep emotion as he roared triumphantly, leapt to a higher ledge, and disappeared into the brush.

The Warriors rushed to the edge of the cliff and peered over, looking for Dr. Shaw, but could see only treetops. Tyler picked up his knife, the carving, and the gun.

He turned to his friends and said grimly, "Let's go see what happened to him."

As they made their way down the cliff, Tyler told them how Shaw found out about their Indian discoveries when he talked in his sleep. He recounted the events that led up to the jaguar attack, leaving out no detail of the ambush in which the evil man had attempted to steal the carving. Tyler also explained that this was the same man he previously reported for killing the jaguar in southern Arizona.

"Wow, what a freaky coincidence. Do you think he's dead?" asked Colter.

"I don't know," responded Tyler. "He sure got chewed up."

Makoa angrily stated, "He deserved it. He pulled a gun on you."

At the base of the cliff, the Warriors followed cautiously behind their leader. They walked back and forth below the spot where Dr. Shaw went off, but caught no sign of him.

"Hey, here's a trail of blood spots!" said Colter. "Looks like they lead to the creek."

After searching for over an hour, they found no more blood or other evidence of the doctor. Too spooked to look around any longer, Tyler and the Warriors nervously returned to camp.

Hidden by overhanging grape vines, they talked in low voices about what should be done and wondered if Dr. Shaw could possibly be watching them from some hidden spot.

"What do you think he'll do now?" asked Makoa. "I know it sounds mean, but I hope the jaguar goes after him. He ruined everything."

"If he's able to, I'm sure he's limping his way back to the campground," said Tyler.

"He could be lying somewhere, too injured to walk," said Colter, "or even bleeding to death."

"That's possible," Tyler agreed. "Your parents are never going to believe this story."

Shawnee asked, "What should we do? If we report him to the police, everyone will find out about the cave and everything."

"I don't know what we're going to do about the cave," Tyler admitted. "We'll have to tell the police and get Shaw some help, better yet, arrested. He may come hunting for us later. Let's just hope something will work out. What a mess."

"He'll probably find a hiker to help him," added Makoa.

"Well, let's first return the carving to its home in the cave," Tyler suggested. "Come with me in case he's still around. Then we'll head up to the main campground and alert the police. Come on – bring your goggles!"

They crept cautiously out of camp, keeping a wary eye out for the doctor. Tyler still carried the pistol and held the jaguar carving hidden in his pack. At the edge of the pool, he hid the gun stealthily in some tall grass after looking everywhere for signs of Dr. Shaw. Tyler camouflaged his actions by simultaneously preparing his goggles and flashlight. He had wrapped the carving in a shirt to sneak it into the water with him. Tyler took one final glance up at the high trail.

"Get down!" he hissed, urgently. "There's Shaw; don't let him see us."

The doctor could be seen limping along the trail above with the help of some tourists, his head bandaged. They passed from view as Tyler and the Warriors slipped beneath the surface of the water.

The sun no longer shone directly on the pool, but everyone made it through the darkened tunnel and up into the cave. The group walked through the fantasy land of sparkling drops glittering everywhere and headed straight for the circle of arrowheads.

Gathering together out of the cold water, they caught their breath. By now, their senses were stunned; nobody said a word. Tyler prepared to take the jaguar carving back through the narrow beaver tunnel, but he wanted a brief rest and felt no great need to hurry.

The Warriors sat down, leaning against the sturdy stalagmites. Four of these pillars topped with embedded arrowheads provided each young adventurer with a convenient backrest. Water drops containing calcium carbonate leached from limestone fell in rapid succession, hitting the arrowheads. With every drop, the adventurers felt a light spray.

They needed time: to let the trail clear and to calm their nerves. As their leader, Tyler knew they would benefit from a temporary mental distraction. He explained that waiting in the cave for things to settle down was probably best.

He settled in, still holding the jade carving, and started a wandering science lecture.

"The Maya believed the drops from a dripping stalactite to be sacred. They often used them in ceremonies," he began. "Stalactites and stalagmites are studied by paleoclimatologists to see past patterns of rainfall. Tree rings can show trends in climate a few thousand years ago, but these cave formations can show trends of 500,000 years or so, if they're big and old enough."

Quiet and in a mild state of shock, none of the Warriors even thought about the cold.

Makoa broke the silence, “They’re sort of like time capsules from the past. The Maya knew they were special.”

Shawnee cut in, "Did jaguars live in the Grand Canyon in the past?"

Tyler answered, “I've read that they did range this far north."

"What about saber-toothed cats?” asked Colter. “Did they ever live here?"

Absentmindedly, Tyler slowly said, “Yeah... the term Smilodon refers to an animal with teeth shaped like a double-edged knife. These large cats lived in North and South America until about 10,000 to 11,000 years ago.

"The larger southern species of this ancient time weighed in at 800 or 900 pounds with slender, serrated fangs measuring 11 inches or more. The North American species weighed between 400 and 600 pounds and possessed fangs or upper canines measuring closer to seven inches.

“Other big cats called this area home, too, including the American lion and possibly even a giant jaguar.

“At the end of the ice age there were giant, something like eight- to 12-foot-tall sloths that lived in caves. Paleontologists have also found remains of teratorns, the largest known living birds. The name means 'monster bird'; the ones in the Southwest had from 12- to 16-foot wingspans. In South America, some of these creatures’ wings could span up to 26 feet!

Makoa spoke up, “I’ve heard of those. They’re kind of like condors but bigger and with narrower, sharper beaks. From what I remember, they were also more of a predatory type of bird. I heard that some Teratorn skeletons were found within the Grand Canyon at Stanton's Cave, near a spring called Vasey’s Paradise in Marble Canyon.”

Tyler nodded, “Yup, right next to the Colorado River.”

While listening to Tyler, all of them stared into the middle of their circle, focusing on a single consistent drip from a stalactite landing in a depression of cave pearls. Tyler impulsively took the jaguar carving and placed it directly under the dripping water.

Makoa tipped his head back, closed his eyes, and said dreamily, "Imagine giant teratorns flying between these huge canyon walls."

In the dark, quiet cave, removed from any outside disturbances, Tyler and the Warriors could easily imagine the past and conjure up visions of these giant predatory scavengers flying up the river and around towering cliffs. All of them simultaneously envisioned this scene from years ago. Tyler started to feel increasingly strange, weak, and unsure. A sense of foreboding came over him, as if his destiny wavered back and forth on a knife blade. He could not have known why; his sixth sense told him the feeling was not just from the traumatic experience with Dr. Shaw.

Something else was coming, vague and mysterious, like mist creeping over a swamp. The Warriors' heads started to tip forward.

For a few moments, they quietly listened to the haunting sounds of the dripping, echoing drops from the stalactites and continued visualizing teratorns and other animals of the last ice age, right here in the Grand Canyon.

Their eyes clouded, as though on the verge of blacking out. Blurred motion seemed to surround them, like being caught in the eye of a hurricane. They collectively anticipated something ominous.

Then a moment later, their sight began to return; everything seemed normal. Looking around at each other, they excitedly burst out talking and quickly realized that everyone had shared the same sensations.

Tyler abruptly interrupted, "The arrowheads are gone!"

Not only that, but the stalagmites that had held the arrowheads now stood half as tall as before. In fact, a great deal of the cave had changed.

"Something's happened," Tyler said. "Let's get out of here!"

He quickly hid the carving behind some rocks. Unnerved, the Warriors rushed over to their escape route but noticed that the underwater tunnel was much bigger and the water much colder. Tyler didn't hesitate; he jumped in to lead the way.

The tunnel seemed to angle down deeper, and the long swim back to the surface strained the capacity of their lungs. Finally surfacing, they swam toward shore as fast as possible through the numbingly cold water.

They paused in shock halfway across the pool; juniper trees crowded the bank instead of the usual ash, cottonwood, and willows. Everything around them had changed.

A large shadow passed over them. The Warriors looked up to see a gigantic bird blocking out the sun. It carried a small horse.

"That was huge!" squeaked Makoa, with a high voice. "It looked a lot bigger than an eagle or condor: more like a teratorn!"

They swam to the bank and pulled themselves up.

"What's happened, Tyler?" cried Shawnee, visibly shaken. "The canyon's all different! Where are we?"

Colter shook his head in bewilderment. "This can't be happening!"

A piercing scream echoed far up the canyon. Instinctively shrinking with fear, their minds raced at the primeval sound. They grouped close together and glanced at one another before staring at the distant cliffs from which the animal cry had come. There, atop a high ledge a good quarter of a mile away, stood a full-grown saber-toothed tiger. Its ivory-like fangs shone unmistakably in the bright sunlight. Sensing that he had been seen, the cat turned his bobtail toward them and crept out of view like a sulking house pet.

At this point, no one doubted they had landed deep in the past.

"That sure looked like a...a saber-tooth," Colter stammered.

Nobody questioned him. In fact, no one could say a thing – everyone just stared off with wide eyes. It surely seemed that somehow they had traveled back in time.

Tyler looked at the river as if expecting an explanation. Watching a large chunk of wood being whipped around in the current, he meekly said, "I feel like that piece of driftwood; there is nothing we can do. A larger force is guiding us."

This "force" had actually brought Tyler closer than ever to his heart's desire, the chance to live in the natural world during the distant, primitive past. However, his heart suddenly ached for loved ones.

He felt a strong separation, even though he couldn't comprehend fully what was going on.

"Let's return to the cave," he said. "We have just enough light on the pool to make it. We've got to try to get back."

As he said this, he wondered to himself, 'back from where?'

Deep in his soul, he could feel the curiosity of the adventurer and the lure to explore this new world more deeply. However, the time had come for action, even panicked action to return to their familiar lives and sense of security. Subconsciously he knew there was no turning back, at least not in the near future.

The Warriors, half frozen, stood for a few more moments as if turned to stone, but Tyler gave an ear-splitting "war cry" having the same effect as the snap of a whip over a team of horses. Back into the cold pool they plunged.

Saber-tooth

Pete Connolly

8

Hunted by the Saber-Tooth

Living in the past
with cultures of old
would be incredible
for us to behold.

So many dangers
would take their toll,
but so much richer
would be our soul.

We miss our loved ones,
That is the truth
as we're hunted
by ol' Saber-Tooth.

Back in the cave and urgently feeling the need to return, they tried to re-create the scene which had transpired before being swept into the past. However, the water drops echoing everywhere seemed to only signal the newer, fantastical time with a repeating message: "Be here now."

The companions sat in the stalagmite circle with Tyler holding the jaguar carving as before. Since to journey backward in time, they had all been thinking about the past, the idea now was to think of the time they came from. All of them concentrated while Tyler talked about the Grand Canyon as they knew it. Nothing happened. Despite trying to deeply visualize the landscape and animals, nothing changed. It was getting late in the afternoon. Tyler, apparently lost in thought, walked over to one of the larger stalactites in the room and put his hands out to catch a drip of water.

Letting it run through his fingers, he said aloud to himself, "The Maya used water from dripping stalactites for ceremonies." Then he turned to the Warriors, adding, "There's Maya markings on the jaguar." Feeling cold and needing to retreat, Tyler announced, "We can't stay here any longer; it's getting late."

They swam back through the tunnel and reached the shore, frozen to the bone, unable to think straight, and in great need of shelter and warmth. Dusk was turning into night, and since the group wore nothing but swimsuits and carried no more than their goggles, one waterproof flashlight, and the carved jaguar, their situation quickly grew desperate!

For a moment they all stood on the bank, physically shivering and mentally paralyzed from the combination of the cold, shock, and fear. Knowing he had to do something to get warm, Tyler started jumping around. His blood started to flow, and while dancing and gazing off, he spotted some cave-like overhangs down canyon that could serve as possible shelter for the night.

He exclaimed, "Look at those overhangs! Maybe we can camp there tonight." Keeping his eyes averted from the Warriors and not daring to let them see his fear, he started off hopping barefoot across the cold river stones. The others spurred themselves into action and followed. The first overhang was too small. Tyler spotted a depression of leaves and other forest litter. He thought about covering themselves with this debris to attempt to keep warm, but instead decided to move on in search of better protection.

After progressing a short distance, Colter stopped and pointed noiselessly at the ground.

Tyler, observing the huge tracks imprinted in the dirt, disturbingly stated, "That could be from a short-faced bear, able to run 40 miles per hour and to grow up to fifty percent larger than brown bears. They are known as one of the most powerful predators of the Ice Age." The Warriors shrank at the thought of such a monster.

The friends continued cautiously down to the next overhang with barely enough light to see. Tyler thought he saw something dart behind a rock and glanced uneasily upstream. He didn't say anything, though immediately thought of the saber-toothed cat. A bird flew out of a bush, and they all nervously sprang like gazelles before moving on silently. Their ears became alert to the slightest sounds, as they had themselves become prey. The next overhang looked promising with dark cave-like openings appearing in the back along the cliff. As they drew near, the startling sound of rocks rustled behind them. A sharp glance over the shoulder revealed an enormous saber-toothed cat launching from its stalking position into a full charge.

"Hurry!" yelled Tyler while leaping toward the closest cave opening, where a thick wall of growling, moving fur barred his entry. A giant sloth had emerged suddenly from the large cave like a giant trap door spider. Tyler ducked into another opening a few yards to the side while the Warriors dodged the sloth and instantly rushed to join him.

Colter, who brought up the rear, screamed as he felt searing hot pain after registering the flash of claws; the saber-tooth had made a last reach, raking the boy's arm. Thick dust kicked up during their flight blinded the adventurers as unearthly savage snarls and growls came from the fighting beasts at the cave's entrance.

The ripping and tearing of flesh coupled with repeated guttural growls of the cat inspired a quick retreat down the tunnel. Tyler flicked on the flashlight as they worked their way farther back. After about thirty feet, the passageway became larger.

"Smell that?" Tyler inquired. "I bet this is an animal's den, probably belonging to the sloth." They soon reached a dead end, a round room carpeted with dried grasses and matted fur. While the odor was strong, it was not offensive. The Warriors pointed out a ledge just above the nest, and they nimbly climbed up onto it. Out of any other options, the group would almost be out of the ferocious feline's reach. Colter's deep scratch, though painful, stopped bleeding after Tyler ripped the pocket from his swimsuit to press over it.

With tears in her eyes, Shawnee lifted her head to ask Tyler, "Do you have the carving?" Despite the complex emotions, her face showed a knowing smile, like a little bit of sunshine with rain.

Tyler, still catching his breath, simply nodded. All of them, tired, scared, and shocked, just lay there motionless in the dark. After many minutes of battle, the snarling and growling finally stopped, and only an occasional scuffling noise reached the ears of Tyler and his friends.

Then a profound silence fell on the cave. The sound of each adventurer's breathing instinctively diminished, dropping to the volume of a lizard's breath.

Tyler and the Warriors, huddled quietly together for warmth on the uncomfortable ledge, prayed that the winner wouldn't come back to the den. Their bare skin froze where it touched the rock, and they eyed the dried grass on the floor of the den. It was hard to stay tensed up and quiet for so long. Tyler felt like a trapped animal about to make a foolish dash for freedom, but he and the others managed to patiently wait out the long night. After a couple of hours, they snatched up a few handfuls of the matted grass to rest on.

Eventually, a weak light reached their cave recess, and knowing it must be daylight, they moved out cautiously. The animals were gone. Following drag marks to a pile of leaves showed the results of the fight. The saber-toothed cat had eaten a portion of the sloth and covered the rest with brush and leaves. As hunger gripped their stomachs, the humans stared at the bloody meat and knew that this would be their dinner.

Tyler sat down as if stunned by a club.

"Are we on another planet?!" he yelled with his back turned to the Warriors. Gazing down the iron-walled canyon seemed to evoke the same hard, stark reality in Tyler's inner geography. The worry and responsibility of their shared destiny sent an icy chill into his spinal fluid.

"We have neither teeth, claws, speed, nor technology... only our brains," he moaned, appearing as though he were talking to the rocks. "How can we survive?" His voice sounded strange and far away; the Warriors had never seen him so beside himself. It concerned them greatly to witness their leader expressing feelings of fear and doubt. Tyler stared at the ground and his feet, continuing to ruminate, though he knew full well that the path of self-pity led to mental, then physical weakness.

A small mouse ran out from under the big rock next to him, snatched up a slow-moving insect, and darted away. Tyler thought, 'if a mouse can find a way to survive here, surely we could, too.'

He cast an agonizing look toward the sky with the hope that some invisible power behind the wonders of nature – a power for "good" – that he often hardly believed in, might help them. Tyler exemplified the kind of man that could be bent but never broken.

The Warriors bravely held their tongues; feelings hung in the air like thick smoke. No one thought of anything positive to say and therefore each fought the urge to complain. They all understood the baffling complexity of their remarkable plight. At the same time, these dear friends knew there's nothing worse than a person who grumbles when unwittingly stuck with others in a difficult situation. Tyler cleared his throat, fighting hard not to give in to despair.

"A man has to have hope. He must have faith in something, to succeed," Tyler stumbled to get the words out. He made eye contact with his younger friends, and they instinctively read his heart. As he told a bad joke, Tyler's mouth widened into a faint smile, though moisture showed in his eyes. While some forced slight smiles, all seemed to retreat into themselves – perhaps an even longer journey than the physical one to come. Tyler felt thankful to be blessed with their strength and patience, so he did his best and solemnly laid out a plan.

Colter doctored his wound near the creek. With Tyler's help, he washed the deep cut thoroughly in the clear water, and it showed no signs of infection.

They spent the first morning in this relatively dazed and agitated mood, but they had to work together now for their lives. Makoa and Shawnee made knives by knocking sharp blades off larger "core" rocks in the way of the ancient people. With these blades, the group began the tedious job of skinning what remained of the sloth. They cut some large chunks for a reserve and placed them into a cache under the shade of a boulder by the river. Tyler and Colter constructed the meat cache within the cool damp earth, using heavy flat rocks and green grass to line it. This meat would be eaten or smoked within the next day or so. They set four large roasts aside for eating that night and stripped the rest to hang in a juniper tree not far from the entrance to the overhang where they had set up their camp.

Tyler suggested, "Let's save the sloth's brain and other soft parts so they can be mixed to tan the hide. We'll be wearing this skin, so we better make it comfortable."

The next priority was fire. With their stone knives in hand for cutting and shaping the fire sticks, they went into the nearby woods to gather the proper materials. Fire starting required one fairly straight stick to twirl, as well as a dry piece of wood with a groove cut into its side for the base. This notch would allow the hot sawdust from the spinning stick to fall through the base and onto a pile of tinder: light, dry, easily burnable material.

Getting a fire started, aside from providing the only method to cook their meat and stay warm at night, would also offer some protection from any large carnivores roaming nearby.

The Warriors worked in constant fear of the return of the saber-toothed cat or short-faced bear. At least it was warm that day, a welcome relief after the teeth-chattering cold of the night. By late afternoon, after many false starts, Tyler and Makoa were getting the hang of the fire drill. Thankfully, a steady stream of smoke rose from the pile of black sawdust in the groove produced by spinning the stick into the base-wood. Tyler quickly took the drill stick away and knelt down to blow softly into the sawdust pile, where a tiny coal lay in the center. He continued to blow on the coal while picking up and carefully cradling in his hand the bird nest-like wad of tinder he had laid underneath it. More and more smoke appeared, and finally the "nest" burst into flames as if by magic.

With a yell of joy, Tyler and his friends momentarily forgot their desperate situation. They cooked and ate the tasty sloth meat, skewering the roasts on stout green sticks placed close to the flames. This was their first meal in more than a day, and with renewed strength the Warriors spent long into the evening stripping the rest of the meat and hanging it in the limbs of a juniper tree above the smoke from the fire.

The Warriors learned firsthand that the reality of life at this base level of survival involved never-ending, physically demanding work and struggle. They had little time to grow homesick so far, but night was drawing near.

Tyler had been hustling to bring in firewood, and already deep shadows filled the canyon bottoms as the upper cliffs glowed with golden light. When settling into their camp, he told everyone about the teratorn he saw while collecting wood.

"It might have a nest nearby," he concluded. Nobody seemed to listen; the Warriors stared listlessly into the fire. Tyler, gnawing on a bone, stopped talking and placed a log on the fire. His eyes glowed with reflected light as he focused his attention on the blaze. It dawned on him that already they had accomplished something greater than simply finding food and making fire. Their own resourcefulness, beyond his expectations, now seemed evident and at their command.

When darkness fell, unfortunately so did their mood. The fire carved its own cave of light in the dark canyon as the travelers worked determinedly to sharpen stout spears with their rock tools.

The sloth's skin had been soaked in water, then coated with a mixture of wood ash and water. The Warriors rolled up the hide and placed it near the cliff, but still close enough to their fire to help keep predators away. They also stacked heavy logs and rocks on top of it.

They planned on sleeping atop the grass and fur "mats" from the sloth's nest and placed them on the ground. Earlier in the day, they had shaken out the mats and smoked them to kill any bugs and to keep others from moving in.

The group prepared to rest for the first time at about two o'clock in the morning, but Tyler stood up for one last chore. He collected the head of the sloth, climbed to a top branch of the juniper tree overhanging the fire, and stuck the animal's head on the end of a stout, pointed snag to keep it from any animals. He climbed carefully down past the drying meat and placed the jaguar carving in the fire's flickering light.

He turned to the Warriors and asked, "What do you think about going back to the cave again?"

No one replied. Tyler looked at the pictures on the bottom of the carving.

"I wonder what the significance of the jaguar pyramid is," he said aloud.

Again, he was met with silence. The Warriors had fallen asleep, totally exhausted, with their spears in hand. Tyler felt fearful of the saber-tooth's return and rekindled the flames every hour throughout the remaining night. Each of them experienced regularly interrupted sleep, because while the side of the body facing the fire stayed warm, the other side froze, and one had to constantly turn from side to side.

During the long, restless night, the Warriors awoke often and resumed their worry that they might forever remain trapped in the past and not able to return. Fitful dreams caused them to thrash about and moan.

In the morning, they were hungry, cold, tired, in foul moods, and arguing over what to do next, how much wood to put on the fire, and everything else.

"What if we can't ever return?" asked Shawnee, tears welling in her eyes.

Colter hugged her close as Tyler reminded his young companions of the need to have faith.

He said plainly, "We have no choice but to do our best with what we have and figure out what needs to be done for the immediate future." They settled down and started talking about the smallest comforts which they longed for: the warmth of their homes, pets, friends, and family. Each vowed to appreciate everything more if they ever got back.

Over the next few days, Tyler and his friends worked vigorously with chores like gathering firewood and building rock defenses They partially sealed the opening to the sloth's cave to use for a hideout as a last resort. The meat-smoking racks required constant tending, and each attendant enjoyed the reward of nibbling away at the cooked meat.

Tyler found time to construct a backrest with small branches and the others also made improvements around camp. Living within nature's flow in the great outdoors stimulated and strengthened them. The Warriors began to feel at ease and could not help but be amazed amidst the incredible scenery, huge canyon walls, and fantastic rock formations. Their friend Tyler had truly led them on an out-of-this-world adventure. All this kept them from thinking of home too much.

The group always worked together for safety and kept their spears and clubs near at hand. Each Warrior carried three fire-hardened spears at all times for protection. They only traveled limited distances from camp because of their bare feet. In truth, the overhang where they built the fire represented their only secure base.

Tyler led the effort to treat the sloth's hide. The hard-working team removed it from its wood ash soak, stretched it over a log, and set to work scraping off the hair using their rock tools. Next, they placed the hide along with the brain of the animal into a natural basin of bedrock full of water. The Warriors took turns stirring the mixture and rotating in some hot rocks from the fire to warm the water. After dipping and wringing out the skin several times, Tyler suggested rolling it up again and putting it aside for a day.

The following day, the entire group stretched the hide out on the bedrock with rocks placed on the sides to hold it down. When it dried, they draped it over the smoking fire on a frame of sticks until the color changed. This process of smoking the skin would enable it to get wet without becoming stiff when dried again and would also keep insects from eating it. After all of this, to make the material more supple, they broke it down by rubbing in sloth fat with smooth, round river rocks. The dedicated bunch eventually succeeded in crafting four crude vests from the hide.

As time went on in the otherworldly wilderness, gathering and breaking up firewood stayed a constant necessity. The creative minds of the Warriors devised games out of this chore by snapping logs between tree trunks and jumping or throwing rocks down on them, but it still amounted to hard, muscle-building work.

The youngsters worked to perfect their fire-starting technique each evening, and before long they had earned their way to a good collection of fire drilling tools as well as hard, callused palms. Of course, the most time-consuming job was finding food. Luckily, the sloth meat they had smoked and stored near the cold river stayed fresh and safe to snack on for several days.

One evening, Colter was checking on that meat cache when he saw a massive lump of dark fur in the bushes. He glimpsed a giant paddle-like tail dragging behind and identified the creature as a beaver, but he could not believe the size of it – almost seven feet long!

Colter called to his friends, "Hurry!" and Tyler and the other Warriors rushed over immediately, weapons in hand.

"Quick, he's going into the grass! Circle around," urged Makoa.

Brandishing their spears and clubs, the team brutally bested the poor animal. The Warriors surprised themselves with their own vicious attack and felt bad for the beaver. It did make for quite a feast, and they also managed to make four pairs of simple moccasins and a small collecting bag from the beaver's thick skin.

Shawnee took a few of the sloth's bones and the tip of an antler found not far from camp and ground them to sharp points on some sandstone to craft awls used for stitching. The moccasins, though crude, felt like such a comfort that the Warriors hunted the creek shore constantly to get more skins. The friends spotted river otters in small groups but found these mammals too elusive and cute to take, and therefore simply watched them swim. Before too long, they cornered another beaver on land and used it to make spare moccasins and another bag.

One day, Tyler and his crew went on a collecting trip to fill their bags with blueberries, piñon nuts, and grass seeds. While napping in the warm sun atop a slope under the cliffs, they observed a group of white mountain goats high on the towering rocks. The overall colder climate throughout this period in the past made the canyon an ideal habitat for mountain goats. All seemed peaceful for the goats, until a dark shadow passed over them; two large teratorns sailed into the scene. A young goat had been lying among the big rocks where the giant birds landed. Sounds of a quick struggle rang out, then the birds flew swiftly away, one of them carrying the now dead mountain goat.

"I hope they drop it for us," Tyler wished, his stomach grumbling.

Before long, on a warm day, everyone felt ready to return to the underwater cave and make another attempt to get back. Just as they reached the middle of the pool in preparation to dive under, the saber-toothed cat reappeared. The predator approached the shore and sniffed the ground. The Warriors' timing could not have been better; like a group of river otters, they dove for the cave, fortunately unseen.

Once inside the cavern, the group spent half an hour trying to figure out how to travel forward to their own time. Despite their varied efforts, nothing was working, and it was growing dangerously cold.

Tyler and the half-frozen Warriors swam out of the cave, warily looking around for the saber-toothed beast, then crept onto shore, ready to jump back in at any moment. The ferocious cat was nowhere to be seen, so the adventurers dashed back to their fire as fast as they could.

The Warriors now made sturdy hooks from the bones of the slain sloth, and they fabricated fishing line out of thin rawhide strips that Tyler demonstrated how to tightly twist, stretch, braid, and cure. These strands needed to be strong enough to handle the real possibility of inordinately big fish.

Wanting to try out their homemade hook and line, they packed the last of the dried meat for a hike down the creek to the Colorado River. However, since the Colorado roared with glacial melt from the north, it proved to be too swift in current and full of sediment for good fishing. They instead worked the mouth of the side canyon where the water was clear and caught two huge squawfish, each around five feet in length. While cleaning these fish, hungry eyes watched the humans. Across the river a pack of dire wolves observed everything. Thankfully, the wolves trotted on after the Warriors had caught them staring at the unreachable feast. After this encounter, the fishermen instinctively ducked under an overhang to finish the cleaning process.

"Would the wolves attack us if they could?" asked Colter.

Tyler replied, "I don't know. Dire wolves are the size of gray wolves from our time, but they weigh more and have larger teeth. They once roamed all over North America." "With fire and weapons to scare them off, we should be able to hold our own."

After they had completed the task of cleaning the fish and had filled their beaver skin packs, the friends washed up in the river. Tyler took notice of something washed up on the rocks, likely delivered by a flood. There on a ledge lay a juniper log measuring six feet long and five inches in diameter.

"I'm going to make a bow with this," Tyler claimed. Juniper trees generally did not provide the best kind of wood for a bow, but this piece appeared mostly straight and seemed to be dried the proper amount. The bark still stuck to it, as well.

"Hey, I found a quartz vein!" Shawnee announced, her head under a rock ledge. "We could make necklaces!"

While she collected a handful, Tyler gathered up the log he had discovered. At the same time, Makoa picked up from the beach a hollow, bleached wing bone from a large bird. Years of weathering had cleaned and polished the bone into pure white.

"I think I can make a flute out of this," Makoa pronounced.

At this point the Warriors and Tyler, having grown more accustomed to their situation, underwent a great increase in their optimism. They were not only surviving, but advancing their weaponry and now hopefully even on the way to producing music and art.

When they arrived back at camp, the Warriors placed most of the fish pieces on sticks in the smoke while Tyler cooked some choice slabs laid atop flat rocks over an adequate bed of coals.

Early the next morning, the Warriors went about making yucca fiber strings for their crystal necklaces. Tyler got to work on fashioning a bow out of the juniper branch.

Colter inquired, "Tyler, when did bows get invented?"

"The first evidence is from about 65,000 years ago in Africa, and then the idea migrated to Asia 15,000 years later, then to Europe 3,000 years after that," said Tyler, remembering his research. "Some of the evidence was recorded in pictographs."

"And when did it come to the American Indians?" Colter persisted.

"Well, some bows have been dated in the southwestern U.S. between 200 and 400 A.D, about 1,500 years ago," explained Tyler as he got back to work.

"People have made them with all kinds of wood and even ram's horns. Juniper isn't the strongest of woods to use, harder wood is better, but it'll have to do. I'll make it stronger by backing it with sinew and rawhide."

He continued, "You know, the bow and arrow replaced the atlatl or throwing spear, which came after spears with removable tips and plain spears before that. The atlatl has been around for 30,000 years; it spread widely through Europe roughly 17,000 years ago."

"So now I'm wondering – when did the flute first appear?" broke in Makoa, bent over the wing bone with a pointed rock blade in his hand.

"About 40,000 or 45,000 years ago. Though, it didn't make an appearance in North America until 7,500 years ago. Funny you asked; I had just read that."

"Took a while to get over here, huh," said Makoa, with his head down working.

"We should make an atlatl next," mentioned Colter as he cleaned his teeth with a carved bone toothpick. He went on, "Hey, Tyler, can I cut some strips from the scraps left over from our sloth hide? I want to try and make a throwing sling. Do you think there are enough?"

Tyler nodded while sawing and chopping on the juniper log with a stone axe he had made from a large flake knocked off a river rock. The chipped rock showed a sharp sawtooth edge. He initially started this project by using large rock flakes to split the log in two. Then, he took one of the halves and removed just the thin bark layer, carving no more away from that side. The wood beneath the bark on the back side of the bow had to remain in one piece to flex without cracking. Next, he tapered the ends and sides down toward the tips and worked only on the belly of the bow, leaving the back intact. The center portion he left thicker for strength, as well as for the handle. During any available downtime, day or night, Tyler shaped his bow.

The day after all the fish had been eaten and acute hunger once again started setting in, the entire group set out on a short hike in search of food. Fortuitously, they came upon a fresh, dead bighorn sheep at the bottom of a cliff. Their luck was evidently holding out. Beyond providing meat for the next few weeks, the deceased creature supplied enough hide to make simple shorts that could replace their worn-out swimming suits. In addition, the ram's horns worked well as containers to drink from. Tyler carefully removed the tendons from the animal's legs, which he would dry for use later.

When around camp, Makoa constantly huffed and puffed on his flute, fiddling with the blow hole using a thin rock "knife" and trying desperately to get a sound. His friends noticed that he would often wander off by himself along the edge of the river; the water noise disguised any evidence of his efforts.

Every day they spotted teratorns, condors, and vultures, along with eagles and other birds of prey. One morning, Tyler and the Warriors ventured up into the cliffs to check out a teratorn's nest spotted from below. The group made it to the top of a section of crags right above the bird's suspected position. Colter had made a sling with rawhide from the sloth and practiced launching rocks great distances from their elevation.

"You better stop now; I think we're getting close to the nest," urged Tyler.

Vultures flew within a few yards of the edge of the sheer vertical drop-offs. As the explorers looked down to search for the nest, these skilled sailors glided through the air around the rock face and over the void. They moved like butterflies buffeted by the wind, constantly angling this direction and that.

Finally discovering the nest ledge, Tyler and his pals climbed on top of an overhang. From this vantage point, they could see one big baby teratorn absolutely covered in soft, feathery down. Within an instant, the angry parent came screaming and squawking overhead with its 17-foot wings flapping wildly, forcing their quick retreat. Bunching together and holding spears at the ready helped coax the giant bird to fly off. Tyler had initially thought he might manage to take an egg, but that possibility clearly no longer existed. Looking at the large, strange chick, they sincerely hoped hunger would not drive them to take this young one for food later.

On the way back toward camp, they descended a steep side canyon with a tiny but fast stream bouncing to the bottom via one small waterfall after another. Tyler and the Warriors stopped to rest among the steep falls, kicking back on the rocks. Makoa got up and wandered behind a fold in the cliffs and sat next to the creek. He took the flute from his bag, held it sideways beneath his mouth, and started playing. Makoa heard the mingling of higher notes with deeper ones as the water slapped against the rocks. A natural harmony emanated from the falling water as it broke the surface of small pools below each waterfall. Makoa's mind picked out and locked onto all these fluid sounds, and he began to mirror the pitch and unique variety with rapid finger changes and deft breath control. He closed his eyes and lost himself in the bliss of mind and soul coming together as music.

Tyler and the others started to wonder what Makoa was doing, when they heard these rapturous sounds coming from around the rock. The noises from the stream seemed to be harmoniously multiplying. Tyler and the Warriors felt positively astounded by the symphony; it moved them to stare off into the distance, fully absorbing the infinite. It was that good.

In this way, they continued to grow and survive, weathering many storms in the shelter of the cave, fishing and finding food wherever possible. Each day's work took so much energy that any food quickly disappeared; rationing turned out to be incredibly difficult. They developed a keen sense of the energy fire burning within, kept alive by even the smallest of tidbits, as they lived on the edge of starvation. Rawhide strips from the bighorn were used in making snares and deadfall traps. Occasionally a pack rat, squirrel, or bird fell victim to such a contraption, though these catches provided little meat. Shawnee wanted to help procure food and found an oak log washed down from someplace and began making a second bow on her own.

A few more months passed, and the group revisited the underwater cave countless times, but efforts to return had ended in no success. They found numerous saber-tooth tracks just outside of camp, but since their first run-in, no one had seen the beast.

"He must be coming around while we sleep" Colter reasoned – not a comforting thought. Gratefully, no bear paw prints had appeared in the area. The camp dwellers kept the fire well stoked at night, but with so many strange cries and calls, far-off huffs, grunts, screeches, and an assortment of distant unidentifiable odd noises, sound sleep was unusually hard to come by.

During the middle of the third month spent within this unique canyon's walls, the Warriors were sitting around camp one morning watching Tyler sort through possible arrows. He sighted along ash branches and arrow weed stalks to find straight ones of proper width and discarded any that seemed off. He had nearly finished sorting through the pile and started to ask someone to cut some more...when he gave a twist of the head, cocked his ear to one side, and in a hushed voice whispered,

"Hear that?"

The Warriors strained their ears to listen.

Then again, Tyler said under his breath, "There, hear that?"

"That scraping sound?" questioned Makoa.

"Yes," said Tyler as he rose to his feet. "Come on."

They grabbed their spears and quickly came across two elk trapped in a slick-sided bowl of rock within a small side canyon just upstream from their camp. The elk had probably entered the area to drink from a pool, but now they couldn't get out. Their hooves slipped repeatedly on the smooth rock, and exhaustion from trying to escape had set in. It made for a gruesome experience, but the Warriors alone took them with their spears. They spent the remainder of the day cutting up the slain animals and making many trips carrying full packs to their home base. Now the friends possessed plenty of meat to keep them strong and enough hides to stay warm at night. Once they finished hauling it all back to their overhang, everyone settled in for a long nap.

Before nodding off, Tyler cautioned, "We ought to keep rationing our meat to build a reserve."

The Warriors were already sound asleep.

Tyler watched the vultures sailing among the cliffs. Other than the buzzing of a single fly heard overhead, all else seemed to announce that the whole world was taking a siesta. The weight of the lonely stillness felt almost unbearable, and thankfully Tyler too fell asleep. They slept for hours.

The kids woke up first, giggling and talking quietly. Tyler still dreamt that he lay in his own bed at home, and he tried to keep his eyes closed to hold onto the image for a few moments more. But when the Warriors started laughing uncontrollably with high-pitched and bright voices, his dreams disappeared, popping like foolish bubbles. It made his heart glad to hear the unabated joy of youth.

He propped himself up on one elbow and looked on, realizing how his young friends had hardened, grown, and developed in maturity. He had witnessed them hunt, climb difficult long and steep slopes, face endless hardships head-on, and fight for survival in multiple ways. They were fearless in the midst of these taxing difficulties, and through it all the Warriors had consoled and taken care of each other. When danger seemed to stalk their every move, their sensibilities only clarified and intensified. Even while living in constant proximity to each other, they avoided the obsession of focusing on one another's faults, which has caused the ruin of many friendships. Accepting others unquestionably as the product of each one's own pasts and genes – that was the way of these Warriors.

The following day, everyone assisted with stripping the elk meat and hanging the pieces on the smoke racks. Again, they used a method involving soaking the skins in water and wood ash to help with hair removal.

In similar fashion to the sloth hide, the Warriors bathed the elk skins in a mixture with the animal's brain, stretched the pelts out to dry, and finally smoked them.

Tyler added more sinew from the elks' tendons to that taken and dried from the bighorn sheep and sloth. He could now back his bow for added strength and would still have enough sinew left over for tying feathers and arrowheads onto the arrow shafts. He began this process by soaking the dried strips of tendon to rehydrate them, then laid the strips along the back of the shaped bow with their edges overlapping. Tyler aimed to mainly reinforce the middle section, where it was most likely to break due to stress during use. In his next step, he mixed pine pitch with some charcoal, sawdust, and a lump of beeswax in a warmed bowl-like rock until it became quite sticky. He spread this glue over the sinew and the entire back of the bow. On top of this, Tyler laid down a long strip of rehydrated, pre-stretched rawhide from the elk. With its whole length backed, the bow would now be stronger and more flexible. Shawnee's bow, being constructed of already strong oak, needed no additional backing.

After the few hard days of work around camp, Tyler announced a plan, "Let's go explore that side canyon downstream."

The explorers headed off in high spirits, feeling self-sufficient wearing their skin shirts and shorts and well-rested from a good night's sleep under the warm elk hides. When Tyler observed the Warriors, he could plainly see how nature had entered them. Now strong and alert, their senses heightened like an animal's: eyes quick and sharp and ears keen to the slightest sounds. While moving through their surroundings, they stopped often to listen, using the silence to their advantage.

"I miss Beau running along beside us," Shawnee reminisced. The rest agreed.

Upon reaching the new canyon, Makoa observed, "There are lots of small caves and overhangs here."

Passing one of these openings at ground level, Colter urgently whispered, "Listen!"

Their sensitive hearing picked up a slight scuffling. With spears bristling, the Warriors tried to silently slink past the cave mouth, but just then, a creature with a large blonde, fuzzy head peered over the rocks by the entrance. Another similar critter quickly joined it, then instantly disappeared. The Warriors instinctively moved in closer to check out these blonde-haired creatures with innocent blue eyes.

Tyler warned, “Be careful,” as they all guardedly crept into the overhanging cave, going around the rocks that lined its entrance. Once inside, they encountered baby sloths bobbing up and down like groundhogs: the cutest little things they had ever seen. The Warriors crawled ever nearer, desperately wanting to reach out and touch one but knowingly holding back. The sloths froze initially, but after bobbing their heads like owls for a short while, they started to relax.

The Warriors made themselves comfortable sitting or leaning on rocks. Tyler glanced down between his feet, noticed a rock that looked like an ancient tool, and bent down to pick it up. Next to it lay another nearly identical large, well-used blade worn smooth where one might grip it. It suddenly occurred to Tyler that other people – yes, humans – could be very close by.

“These are stone tools,” he pointed out, noticing that the Warriors’ focus remained on the sloths.

Tyler had known that the Clovis mammoth hunters, also called the Paleo-Indians, allegedly lived in this general region beginning about 11,500 years ago. Evidence showed their arrival in the Grand Canyon roughly 10,000 years ago. He shook his head, having never imagined that they might someday come across people outside of their present group. The Warriors, still observing the sloths, could hardly be distracted. Tyler walked out in front of the cave's overhanging roof to stand watch and sit in the warmth of a narrow strip of sun that had fleetingly found its way into the narrow canyon. Like a curious primate, he inspected the tools in his hands and thought about what would happen if they ran into a group of these people nearby. Would they be friendly or dangerous? If friendly, the relationship should help their odds of survival: they could learn from these people how to hunt big game and learn which plants to use for food and medicine. Of course, the social mix would present the greatest gamble in this situation, due to humans being so particular. Not to mention, the language barrier and different cultural and social ways could further complicate interactions.

The brilliant light on the cliff behind Tyler seemed to help clarify his thoughts. Lately he had carried an additional weight on his spirit that also kept him up at nights: a nagging worry that he and his young friends must move on. Tyler realized that now his subconscious harbored a strong blind feeling that he and the Warriors must follow the map on the belly of the jaguar carving. However, that would mean actually traveling to the jungles of Central America, the land of the Maya, and Tyler knew that the temple shown on the carving would not have existed during the time in which they currently found themselves. The Maya constructed their temples, with flat topped pyramids like the one engraved on the jaguar, between 250 B.C. and 900 A.D. – long after the time period near the end of the glacier days. Though he felt wary and worried about possibly meeting the Paleo-Indians, Tyler also felt a sort of calm simultaneously enveloping him. He recognized within him a hunger for the warmth and security of a "tribe" and the need to be part of a culture. Even in this extremely harsh environment, nature, along with their diligence, had so far always provided them with the bare necessities. On the other hand, within their small group, life seemed to be missing various social complexities that Tyler and the Warriors would before long need to be fulfilled. Tyler's positive feelings about finding the Paleo-Indians likely came from his lifelong dream of living close to nature, side by side with people of ancient cultures. These people might also truly help them to survive, so long as they were accepted. He could only hope that fate would lead him and his companions on a good trail. He decided then and there that they must travel on and fully explore this new world.

Tyler still sat motionless, looking both into his heart and out on the world. The subtle sounds of voices that escaped from under the overhang accentuated the general silence, the loneliness, and the responsibility.

As always when reflecting alone, he thought about loved ones left behind: mostly Sierra, his loving mom, and his dad who had shared so much interest and knowledge of archeology and anthropology with him. He could literally feel his heart straining to reach them and imagined being bound to them by some invisible electrical current--radar love. Like a blind and deaf person who loses these senses but finds others heightened, Tyler realized that his new existence, so withdrawn from the distractions of modern life, allowed him to feel more strongly with his heart than ever before. He was learning to surrender to the powers beyond him. Throughout this rougher period of life, often bordering on suffering, it proved hard to keep positive. Yet even in tough situations, he had managed to keep an ember of faith alive until a breeze of good fortune could come along and ignite that burning hope into a blaze of renewed passion for life.

Tyler remained deep in thought and settled into the earth like a stone. Frightened by these feelings of loneliness and weary of the sense of responsibility that hung over him, he felt the canyon walls staring at him like a stranger invading their territory. After all these years, now he surely looked the dragon straight in the eye and despaired within the cruel depths of these emotions. Apparently, no hope of finding lost ones left behind truly existed, and he felt his love for them painfully left to smolder in his heart.

Thankfully, at that moment a warm, scented spring breeze blew into the canyon, stirring up a flood of good memories from the depth of Tyler's all-feeling heart. Succeeding in his effort to turn off the hard thoughts for now, he perceived his own acceptance of the canyon, and life "as it is." Positive and constructive emotions returned as he reassured himself. The Warriors had never blamed him and adjusted rapidly to their condition. He would have to accept their collective odyssey unfolding one step at a time; like moving along any twisting road of life, one can only see a short distance ahead. A straight line appeared between his eyes that would be chiseled deeper and deeper as time wore on. He keenly reminded himself, as he had taught the Warriors, that if they wished to survive, they must live with constant awareness. Luckily, most of their lives served as great preparation for this.

Tyler jumped up – something was on him! He glanced down and saw one leg already covered with ants. He quickly brushed them off, feeling foolish for already failing an awareness test. Tyler collected his spears and rejoined the others, keeping an eye out in all directions before ducking into the little cave.

He took time to show the rock tools to the Warriors, then fearing the return of the mother sloth, urged his friends on to further explore the side canyon. The canyon climbed constantly upward, and before long it appeared to possibly connect to the top of the rim, however, it was time for them to turn around. On their way back to camp, plans fermented in Tyler's brain.

Under their overhang that evening, Tyler explained his plan for the group to hike out of the canyon, explore the rim, and search for Paleo-Indians.

"Let's take an extended trip," he said. "If we find a better place to survive, great. If not, we'll come back."

"What if we can't find water?" Shawnee asked.

"We'll only travel as far as our water will last, including the return trip, unless we find plenty more," Tyler reassured.

"We'll need to find springs or creeks to keep going" added Colter, enthusiastic about the challenge. Even as he spoke, he put most of his attention on a spear he was shaping.

They decided together that they would embark in a few weeks, though deep inside everyone felt the dread of leaving their secure base.

Over the following days, Tyler and Shawnee worked on finishing their bows and arrows. They each cut out three long strips of rawhide, soaked them and tied the ends to a branch, then stretched, twisted, and braided the strips together for a three-ply bowstring. Tyler showed Shawnee how to use sinew wrapped around the middle of the string where the arrow would notch and around the loops that fit on the ends of the bow to make these areas stronger. They even coated the bow strings with wax from an abandoned beehive for longer wear.

Work such as this continued for a couple of days: wrapping feathers onto arrows using the sinew and either sharpening or serrating fire-hardened wood points of arrows and spears. Their stone arrowhead chipping skills were not sufficiently mastered yet.

Soon the two archers stood armed with seven arrows each, carried in bighorn sheepskin quivers. They practiced daily by holding shooting contests and aiming at soft decaying trees or taking high shots at the cliffs with reject arrows. Even though Tyler and Shawnee would wield the bows for now until more could be constructed, all of the Warriors practiced shooting with them. It felt good to rally together around their goal, to prepare for something, and to stay busy.

Many days of preparation passed, and they accomplished every task they could possibly think of. Makoa packed the last of the dried elk meat in crude skin bags. Colter filled water containers, two made from rams' horns with beeswax and bark lids and another two from cured elk bladders. Shawnee poured some sun-dried berries into the beaver skin bags; they could hopefully forage more while traveling.

Spare moccasins would hang from each of their sides, tied tightly in place. Tyler bound up the fire-lighting sticks with yucca rope to sling over his shoulder along with his bow and quiver of arrows. He found a small turtle shell and repurposed it as a box for carrying their collection of fire-starting tinder: dried moss, fine bird nests, and a plant material similar to cotton.

The adventurers prepared their own individual sleeping skin for folding into packs that each would carry. They had readied spears, as usual, and Tyler planned to carry the carved jaguar safely wrapped in his sleeping hide.

They were down to the final night in camp before departing. Everyone slept restlessly, wondering what they'd find outside of the canyon and far from their familiar cave.

The unnerving thought of running into cave bears, saber-tooth cats, or huge packs of dire wolves mentally paralyzed them. Somehow, Tyler and the Warriors had lasted this long, which gave them some confidence. The plan was to move slowly and either find secure camps or retreat.

At first light, they started their trek up the small canyon that appeared to lead to the very top. It became steeper and steeper until late in the day when they reached a section of sandstone cliffs with many overhangs; water seeped through the rock in a few spots here, signaling a good place to find camp. They indeed located a comfortable shelter with a floor of fine white sand, worn from the sandstone. The Warriors could now expertly start a fire and had one going in just a few minutes. The blaze illuminated a wall covered with ferns from a small dripping spring. The Warriors positioned the ram's horn water vessels under the drips while they ate some dried meat and berries; the containers filled in merely an hour's time. When the last bright colors of sunset still highlighted the glowing cliffs, Makoa moved out onto a ledge away from the others to look over the canyon. Since he walked off in a serious and meditative fashion, the Warriors knew he needed a little space. He stood in apparent reverie, looking into the distance, but not merely observing. In fact, he seemed to be feeling, tasting, and completely experiencing the exhilaration of existence – the thrill of "being."

Tyler watched Makoa, envious of his apparent mental freedom. The grown man thought to himself, 'Youth is so adaptable. It does not tend to burden itself with over-thinking, and it lives for the moment when it comes.' Perhaps that is both the strength of youth, and also its downfall. Fear constantly nagged at him these days, like the constant smell of smoke from distant fires. To survive, he must choose passionate, hard work over despair. Tyler tried to redirect his thoughts and consider his fortunate life situation, full of the freedom to explore and experience unspoiled, rich environments with friends. Of course, separation from loved ones and lack of medical help lingered as major concerns, but the only way to realistically approach these problems at present was to "hope for the best."

He thought if he worried too much about the future, he might spoil the present and leave true freedom out of reach. Tyler reminded himself that he needed to stop second guessing what he had done leading up to this point. Their quest had been true and noble, he concluded. These mysteries had found him and the Warriors as equally as the group had searched. He vowed to work toward the future but to live, fully, in the present and to calmly accept the difficulties that inevitably lay ahead.

Leaving Makoa to his meditation, Tyler turned to the other Warriors. They stood together silently and simply absorbed the energy of the moment. After a few loud sighing breaths, they heard high, clear, and sharp notes as Makoa played his bone flute to the canyon. Hoping that they would remain safe among the steep cliffs, Tyler allowed the music. When Makoa finished the short song, the tired climbers nestled into their camp.

Up early the next morning with the horn canteens and bladders full, they ascended the cliff: a vertical wall of cracks and ledges. This process took all morning and included a good deal of route finding and backtracking.

The four comrades ate lunch on a large ledge at the top while two falcons dove over them in a high-speed aerial show. Just beyond their perch stood a slope leading to a section of worn-down cliffs, seemingly easier to negotiate. The Warriors led the way toward the incline, reached the steeper rock, and worked through an area of small, wind-carved sandstone caves.

When the young journeyers came over a giant boulder, they immediately stopped in their tracks, crouched like birds with their eyes wide and mouths open as they panted out of breath. Within a few seconds, Tyler caught up and found himself also staring ahead at four human skulls lying among a scattering of bones. A closer investigation revealed a broken-off fang from a saber-toothed cat tucked beneath an overhang. The tooth looked viciously sharp, knife-like, and serrated along its edges.

After poking around the area and lining up the skulls to "look" out over the canyon, the group walked off a short distance and looked back at the scene once more. The skulls took on a horrible significance; the Warriors instinctively imagined their own skulls lying somewhere, bleached white with hollow eyes. Shuddering with the fear of now fully confronting this dangerous world, a weakness fell over them. As Tyler and his friends continued, their knees sagged heavily and their heads hung low.

Tyler attempted to encourage them, "We've got to have faith in the world and life, with all its mysterious ways."

"Life is...awesome, and I guess, still 'good' in general," threw in Shawnee.

"Yeah, even though bad things happen, we see a lot of good and amazing things," said Colter.

"There's more that's good, I'm sure, in living – for most people," added Makoa.

"Especially for those who can appreciate the world's common miracles," concluded Tyler.

The explorers needed to hold onto blind faith as their power to overcome adversity and not give up. Those seeking fulfilling lives cannot allow the often-brutal ways of the world to wither away at their dreams and goals. Realizing that really no other choice existed but to keep cheerfully trying, Tyler and the brave youths forced themselves to stand tall and pulled it together for the final steep climb out of the canyon. The ascent through the limestone rimrock felt so precipitous that the general ban on swearing somehow naturally went overlooked in a most hilarious and experimental way. For the most part, Tyler set an example by refraining from slovenly language. However, he knew that the Warriors experimented with "free speech" at their age, and after talking to them at great length, he left them to find their own equilibrium in this matter.

After climbing the last of this steep section, they collected a few fossils and then "topped out." Bright green indicated seeping water ahead. A lush meadow bordered by a beautiful forest of junipers greeted the jubilant travelers. The last of the canyon's strong rim winds had trailed them so far, but finally started to let up.

Colter, who led at the moment, looked over his shoulder and said to Tyler and the others, "Should we keep going this way?"

Tyler waited for the wind to die down and answered rather harshly, "Follow the draw to the top of the hill."

The long meadow leading up the hill was covered with bright blooms of Indian paintbrush waving in the breeze. Colter launched a practice throw with his sling; the big rock landed with a funny "thunk" as though it had hit a rotten tree. The thick brush moved erratically, disturbed by something apparently slinking off. The dense undergrowth on the side of the meadow kept the Warriors from following. Two black ravens flew low through the wonderfully clear air. The simple joy of sweeping one's eye over such country was exhilarating, and the adventurers' minds brimmed with the beauty of each step. The bright green grass, brilliant flowers, deep blue of the sky, and last sections of scattered colorful rimrock all bewitched them.

The heaving of Tyler's heart coupled with the riot of exhilaration in his body and soul at such a brilliant moment forced a sharp victory cry from his lungs. He looked to the sky and cried out in jubilation. The sound seemed to come not from him, but from the air itself. Tyler led the way; his mind now wandered far before him as he reveled in the beautiful surprises of nature. Introspectively realizing he still harbored fear of survival, he also recognized that the deep and quiet parts of his soul grew more at ease the longer he spent in the wilderness. With his thoughts uncluttered, he could "see" more of the wonders around him. Each passing day, he became more used to the type of life that man and all animals were designed for – adventure mixed with peace, awareness, and self-defense. He felt ready to instantly react to countless changes in his environment, more alert to sights, sounds, smells, touch, and intuitive feelings than ever before. He and the Warriors had wrestled with an odd mixture of emotions throughout the last months, experiencing regret and bewilderment alongside joy and fulfillment. They weathered bouts of frightening cold shivers and had enjoyed at other times an enveloping warm thankfulness. Tyler felt the joy of youth, or primitive man, having built forts and camps, fashioned weapons from the most basic elements, and only eaten what they could obtain from nature. He did feel victorious.

A large hawk flew into the big pine tree overhead; a squirrel still struggled in its talons. With a look of wild fury in its eyes, the bird of prey watched the travelers pass below. Tyler's introspection ended.

Every Warrior picked up the pace, growing elated at the verdant ground they now easily traveled. Unfortunately, their impression of wellbeing could hardly have been more misleading. While consumed with awe of the natural beauty all around, they were also being watched and analyzed as potential enemies.

Walking east, with the afternoon sun warming their backs, the group came to the top of the hill and gasped at what they witnessed below. A huge valley spread out before them; there in the middle near a marshy lake – no mistaking it – sat a camp of Paleo-Indians. Massive gleaming mammoth tusks supported skin tents, and a group of ten to twelve skin-clad people gathered around what looked like two young penned-up bison.

Tyler and the Warriors were simply too scared and astonished to move; the Indians already looked their way. No time remained to run or seek cover; armed skin-clad warriors had already stepped out along their route to flank the new arrivals, four or so on each side. The moment left no room for weakness. The survival of the adventurers now depended entirely on their actions and attitude. Tyler felt guilty that he had failed to be more cautious coming over the unexpected summit, but it also seemed as though their trackers had been onto them for a while.

Instinctively having faith that he and his beloved friends were meant for more on this earth, Tyler squelched his fear. 'Why else had they found such secrets and endured so much?' he thought. It seemed a near miracle.

A flash of clarity burst upon his brain; the magnitude of their adventure in terms of both exploration and science suddenly seemed incredibly wonderful. His father and mother would be so proud of him. How had they gotten this far?

As this rush of awareness came over him, Tyler saw his lifelong dream of living in the distant past with its wild freedom and mysterious primitive people being fulfilled. As if caught in a trance, his eyes became like alien glass orbs. His mind shut down all rambling thoughts to allow for full sensory and visual awareness, seeing all in front and to the sides. He felt ready for battle, while at the same time he mentally gathered these people into his soul, with the goal to accept each and every one of them and to give away the most valuable treasure man can give: love.

With a soft, inspired voice he encouraged the Warriors to have strength. Acute feelings of danger, curiosity, and wonder worked through his excited brain. Writhing nerves snaked up and down his spine. Yet, surprisingly, confidence overpowered fear in a way that he could hardly understand.

As they walked on, the Warriors felt his vibe and strived for confidence of their own. The struggle to survive the last few months had hardened them as much as their quartz pendants sparkling in the sun. Colter's long blond hair, hanging loose and shining brightly, must have inspired an additional sense of wonder in the eyes of the Indians. Down into the valley the Warriors and Tyler bravely went, with peace in their hearts, wide eyes, and every sense alert.

A loud flock of geese suddenly came over the hill, a hundred feet or so up in the sky. Tyler unexpectedly fitted an arrow and let it fly. A fat goose tumbled out of the air in front of them. He picked it up by the long neck and slung it over his shoulder. A second flock approached, squawking loudly, and Shawnee boldly followed Tyler's example, instinctively raising her bow to full draw. Amazingly, the arrow squarely hit a second goose, and it fell, pinned through the breast. Behind them, they heard the sounds of falling water. Makoa had taken out his flute. At the far end of the meadow, the Paleo camp stood transfixed as they watched the apparently fearless approach of these strangers.

The End

ABOUT THE AUTHOR

G. C. Grange in His "Warrior" Days - Author G. C. Grange is a wilderness explorer and adventure guide with more than fifty years' experience traveling the remote rugged lands of wild Arizona and the West.

www.ingramcontent.com/pod-product-compliance
Ingram Content Group UK Ltd.
Pitfield, Milton Keynes, MK11 3LW, UK
UKHW022024190726
13853UKWH00005B/2095